MICHEL LEVESQUE's
ARIELLE QUEEN
BOOK I - A KNIGHT FOR A QUEEN

TRANSLATED BY
GREG KELM

8th House Publishing
Montreal, Canada

Copyright © 8th House Publishing 2015
First Edition

Published worldwide by 8th House Publishing.
Front Cover Design by 8th House Publishing
Pendant Design and Back Cover by Simon Bergeron

Designed by 8th House Publishing.
www.8thHousePublishing.com
Set in Adobe Caslon Pro, Dead Saloon and Armalite.

LIBRARY AND ARCHIVES CANADA CATALOGUING IN PUBLICATION

Lévesque, Michel J., 1971-
[Arielle queen. English]
     Michel Levesque's Arielle queen / translated by Greg Kelm.

Translation of: Arielle queen / Michel J. Lévesque.
Contents: Book 1. A knight for a queen
ISBN 978-1-926716-32-9 (pbk. : bk 1)

     I. Kelm, Greg, 1971-, translator II. Title. III. Title: Arielle queen. English

PS8623.E9468A8413 2014   jC843'.6   C2014-908118-9

ARIELLE QUEEN
BOOK I

A KNIGHT FOR A QUEEN

For you, Mariève, the pearl of my heart, with eyes the colour of honey....
- Michel Lévesque

In memory of my aunt and godmother, Pauline Beaudoin, a great lover of the written word in two languages, who passed away on October 7, 2014.
- Greg Kelm

A Knight for a Queen

Simon Bergeron © 2014

Chapter 1
Arielle opened her eyes…

And saw her cat, Brutus, curled up at the foot of her bed. Seeing his owner awake, Brutus got up and stretched lazily in that way cats do. He then padded across the bedspread to Arielle's exposed face, nuzzled her cheek in greeting and turned to settle on the other pillow.

As Arielle lay staring at the ceiling, she savoured the events of the past twenty-four hours. Yesterday had been her sixteenth birthday. Not only had her two best friends, Elizabeth and Rose, treated her to a special girls' night out, she had gotten an unexpected gift that had made this birthday even more wonderful:

The boy of her dreams, Simon Vanesse, had smiled at her for the first time.

Simon and Arielle were grade 10 students at Glory High, where Simon was considered a total hottie by just about every girl at school. Every morning when she woke up, Arielle would picture herself and Simon gazing into each other's eyes. But this fantasy, she glumly admitted to herself, would probably never come true. She felt she just wasn't pretty enough to stand a chance with him. After all, he was tall and good looking and the captain of the hockey team, while she—well, she was short and fat. Her red hair was as frizzy as a ball of steel wool. She had so many freckles, it looked like someone had spritzed her in the face with a can of spray paint.

Suddenly, all thoughts of Simon were swept away by the image of Lea Darling, a stunning beauty who happened to be one of their classmates. Lea was tall and thin, with long, blond hair, bright blue eyes and gleaming white teeth. The tight sweaters she wore showed off her perfect figure.

Arielle was jealous of Lea.

Jealous because Lea was beautiful. Jealous because Lea was graceful and could make heads turn as she glided past. Jealous because people not only found Lea attractive, they wanted to be her friend. Jealous because the teachers smiled at Lea and thought she was smart. Arielle was especially jealous because Lea was Simon Vanesse's girlfriend, and because Lea and Simon would hold hands whenever they were together and would make out every day after class. Arielle really hated that girl. She was everything that Arielle was not.

"Her teeth are all going to rot away with all the junk food she eats!" Elizabeth would whisper every time they saw Lea drinking a can of soda while sitting in the bleachers with her three friends: Daphne Rivers, Judith Monk and Bianca Letarte. The members of this trio all dressed the same way, had the same trendy hairstyle, ate the same thing for lunch at the cafeteria and spoke down to people in the same snotty tone. In the outskirts of the high school social scene, these three girls were referred to as the Carbon Copies, or "CeeCees" for short.

"Arielle!"

The teenaged girl's train of thought was derailed by Uncle Yvan yelling up the stairs.

"Get up, Arielle!" His tone was sharp, almost harsh. But Arielle was used to it.

"Coming!" she replied, looking at her alarm clock. It was 7 a.m. The bus would be there at 8.

The drawn curtains made her room rather dim. Arielle threw off the covers and was about to swing her legs onto the floor when she noticed a shadowy form in the corner of the room. Startled, she thought someone was standing there, but soon realized it was only her uncle's video camera. Perched on top of the tripod, the camera seemed to fix its one eye upon her. Arielle was puzzled—the camera hadn't been there last night when she went to bed.

She then noticed the black cable linking the camera to the small television on her desk. A note attached to the television read:

HAPPY BIRTHDAY!
PRESS PLAY

The handwriting looked familiar. *Uncle Yvan must have written the note,* Arielle thought. Maybe he had woken up after Arielle had gone to bed and had decided to record a message to apologize for having forgotten her birthday. She dismissed the idea; her uncle never felt guilty about anything. But why would he set up the video camera in her room? What did he have to say that was so important that he took the time to record his thoughts in the middle of the night? She was not sure if she wanted to watch the video. After all, Uncle Yvan had been drinking heavily when she got home last night. She was worried that, once again, his behaviour and confused ramblings would be yet another source of disappointment. Seeing him drunk always broke her heart.

Arielle finally got out of bed, curiosity getting the better of her. She wanted to know what the camera had seen and heard, even at the cost of eroding what little respect she still felt for her uncle.

She pressed POWER on the TV and PLAY on the camera before sitting on the bed to watch the show. The screen remained black for a few seconds before suddenly flashing up, as if someone had turned on a light. Arielle recognized the source of the illumination in the video as the lamp on her nightstand. The video had been filmed in her room!

"I know what you're thinking," said a voice that was definitely *not* her uncle's. "But you're wrong."

A woman's voice was coming out of the television. Arielle peered at the screen and saw the silhouette of a figure sitting on a bed—*her* bed!

"After his third bottle of wine, your uncle lay down on the couch and slept there all night. But that's nothing new, huh?" the voice continued. "I'm the one who set up the video camera. I found it in the basement."

The silhouette drew closer to the lamp. Arielle could kind of make out the face. The long black hair and delicate features confirmed the figure was a woman. She seemed young. Her blouse and pants were black, as was her long leather coat.

"I need your help, Arielle," she said. "Tonight."

Her help?

"I'm getting weaker by the hour. I don't have much time." She stopped to catch her breath. "Listen carefully. Tonight, you have to go to bed very early. Do you understand? Look at the pendant I gave you while you were asleep."

Putting her hand to her throat, Arielle located the piece of jewellery. She gently grasped it and pulled it forward to examine it. The pendant was in the shape of a half moon. The inscription on it read: *Fra Retla Fra Alter*. Arielle had no idea what that meant.

"Don't show it to anybody," said the young woman. "I'll be able to speak to you when you wear it."

Their eyes met through the screen.

"I'm counting on you, Arielle. Don't forget: tonight, you have to fall asleep before sundown."

The woman's face was illuminated as she leaned over to turn off the lamp. Staring at the woman's features, Arielle had the strangest impression she knew her.

"Who are you?" she asked, foolishly aware she was speaking to a video recording.

The answer came from a voice inside her.

"I am the shadow, and you are the light."

The teenager pressed PAUSE, and the image froze onscreen. Studying the young woman's features, Arielle realized that the woman looked like her.

But without the freckles.

CHAPTER 2

The bus lurched from side to side…

Creaking and groaning like the hull of an ageing freighter. An encounter between pothole and tire caused the passengers to all bounce in their seats simultaneously. Arielle began to feel sick to her stomach. Not only did she hate taking the bus (even the fifteen-minute ride was too long, in her opinion), the mysterious message from that morning left her confused.

Arielle decided a round of Nursery Rhyme Rewrite, one of her and Elizabeth's favourite childhood games, would improve her mood. Nudging Elizabeth's arm, Arielle said, "I do declare, *Row, row, row your boat* needs a rewrite!" Elizabeth grinned, recognizing their code phrase for the game. Arielle thought for a few moments, licked her lips and recited in a sing-song voice, "Ride, ride, ride the bus, praying you don't crash, rickety, rickety, rickety, rickety, what the?! Look out! SMASH!" Elizabeth burst out laughing, but Arielle's fake-sounding chuckle did not escape Elizabeth's notice.

"Is something wrong, Elle?" asked Elizabeth.

Arielle shifted uneasily.

"Something weird happened this morning," she replied.

"Tell me about it," said Elizabeth, concerned.

In hushed tones, Arielle began her strange tale...

ARIELLE AND ELIZABETH lived in Glory, a little town that owed its name to the morning glory, a colourful flower that unfolds its petals at daybreak and closes them at night. But in the 1920s, the mayor and council decided "the shorter, the better," and the rest, as they say, was history.

Most people in the area worked at the Saturnia hammer factory owned by Xavier Vanesse, Simon's grandfather. The opening of this factory in 1962 had saved Glory from becoming a ghost town populated by a dwindling number of retirees. But Xavier Vanesse needed employees for his factory, so he had hundreds of workers and their families brought in from across the country. And thus Glory was reborn. But Arielle and her uncle, unlike most of the other townspeople, moved to Glory in 1990, only a few months after the death of Arielle's parents.

A PROCESSION of yellow buses braked in front of the school, each discharging its jostling adolescent cargo one after the other. It was cold outside. To reach the main entrance, Arielle and Elizabeth had to wind through the clusters of smokers and the couples playing tonsil hockey.

"Did she say her name?" Elizabeth asked after the two girls were away from the crowd.

Elizabeth Quintal had been Arielle's best friend since primary school.

"No," replied Arielle. "She only said I had to help her."

"Help her do what, Elle?"

Arielle shrugged.

Elizabeth paused, her eyebrows knitting together.

Arielle recognized the first part of her friend's problem-solving ritual. Once Elizabeth had found a solution, she would then tighten the rubber band holding her pony tail and adjust her glasses.

"I'll sleep over at your place tonight," announced Elizabeth, her hair and glasses neatly—and predictably—straightened.

"That's sweet of you to offer, Liz," said Arielle, "I know this is going to sound weird, but I really think I should meet her alone."

Elizabeth's jaw dropped.

"Are you kidding me? What if she tries something?"

The two friends always did everything together, but the woman in the video was something Arielle *knew* she had to handle on her own.

"I'm positive the woman doesn't want to hurt me. And I have this feeling it would be better if no-one else was there when she shows up."

"Why do you say that?"

"I just know, Liz. Please trust me on this one, OK?"

Elizabeth had her doubts; the look she gave Arielle said as much.

"Fine," Elizabeth muttered as she turned away, upset Arielle may be putting herself into danger, and also feeling hurt that Arielle was shutting her out of something important.

Arielle trailed the sulking Elizabeth into the school.

THE TWO GIRLS met up with Rose for their morning classes. Elizabeth was the best student in grade 10 English, while Rose could make the same claim for grade 10 math. Arielle's favourite subject was history, because she found it easy to remember dates. In fact, doing well on a history test was one of the rare things that made Arielle feel special—if only for the time it took her classmates to compare their marks.

Elliot, Rose's boyfriend, joined them at lunchtime. He was in the same morning classes as Simon Vanesse and Noah Davidoff.

"Is Simon here today?" Rose asked Elliot casually as she gauged Arielle's reaction.

Rose was pretty. Elliot wasn't too hard on the eyes either, but he was not nearly as handsome as Simon, even though both boys were blond and blue-eyed. Elliot wore a pair of white Nikes on which he had written Rose's name in a fancy ink mosaic—a personal fashion statement announcing to the world that he was deeply in love with his girlfriend.

"Yeah, Simon's here today," Elliot answered. "He's here every day. Why do you ask?"

"I'm not the one who wants to know," said Rose, smiling sweetly at Arielle.

"Rose!" blurted Arielle, embarrassed.

Elliot turned to her. "What's the big deal? Everyone knows you like him."

"Can we change the subject, please?"

"Aw, we just like seeing you blush," Elliot chuckled.

"Did Arielle tell you what happened this morning?" asked Elizabeth as she took a bite of her sandwich.

Arielle glared at her friend, but Elizabeth took no notice, her attention focused on her bottle of juice. At any rate, Elizabeth knew full well that Arielle did not want to talk about the woman in the video.

"So, what happened?" asked Rose.

Arielle hesitated. Elizabeth kept her gaze locked on the bottle in her hand as she sipped on a straw.

"Tell us!" Rose insisted.

As Arielle turned to respond, she finally caught Elizabeth's eye, shooting her a look that said she wanted to strangle her.

"A woman left a video message for me."

"What did it say?"

"That she needs my help. I don't know why. And she said she didn't have a lot of time left."

"Do you know her?"

"No."

Elizabeth raised her head. "Tell them."

Arielle pursed her lips and gave Elizabeth a swift kick under the table.

"OW!"

Rose snapped her fingers to get Arielle's attention. "Tell them what?"

Arielle sighed. "The woman looks like me, except her face is thinner and she has no freckles."

"Is she some long-lost twin sister you never knew about?" asked Elliot.

"I don't have a sister."

"A cousin, maybe?" he suggested.

"Maybe, but I doubt it."

"What are you going to do?" It was Rose's turn to ask questions.

"Help her, I think. It looks like she's really counting on me."

At that moment, Arielle saw Simon pull open the cafeteria doors. His best friend, Noah, was with him, along with two of their buddies: Oliver Guinness and William Louis-Seize. Noah and Simon had known one another since junior kindergarten and played on the same hockey team. Noah shared Simon's athletic build, but not his charm—nor his good looks.

The four walked up to a table and began talking to another student, a boy Arielle had never seen before. His hair was long, longer than was typical for guys his age, and he wore funny-looking clothes. Simon and he had a quick exchange that did not appear friendly. Suddenly, the unknown youth shot up and pushed Simon. Oliver and William immediately leaped to Simon's aid, placing themselves between Simon and his attacker. A lunchroom monitor hurried over. With a flurry of gestures, the monitor sent the new student away and ordered the other four to scatter.

"That guy's going straight to the principal's office," said Rose, providing post-fight commentary.

Simon and Noah did as they were told and headed in a different direction from their two friends. Arielle's heart began to race as Simon and Noah drew near. Simon walked briskly, looking straight ahead, but Noah began to slow down, apparently searching for something. His face was as impassive as ever, a nasty scar of unknown origin scrawled across his right cheek. Noah was neither ugly nor handsome, and he almost never smiled. Most girls felt he wasn't exactly top boyfriend material. Apparently, he didn't date much.

Noah scanned the cafeteria and stopped when his eyes met Arielle's. She dropped her gaze, embarrassed at being caught staring.

"Noah's coming," Elizabeth whispered.

It sounded like a warning.

Rose and Elliot greeted Noah, but he ignored them. Arielle hesitatingly raised her head as he towered over her.

"Nice pendant," he said evenly.

Arielle immediately looked down and put her hand to the collar of her shirt. To her relief, the pendant was still hanging around her neck, safely out of view.

"Elle, are you OK?" Rose asked, concerned.

Arielle did not know what to say. Noah looked at her for a second before continuing his march to exile from the cafeteria.

"Arielle, answer me! What pendant is he talking

about?"

The plump teenager turned to Elizabeth and Rose, her mind spinning.

I never showed it to anyone, she thought frantically. *How could he have known I was wearing it?*

AFTER HER LAST class, Arielle went to get her things. Elizabeth had already put on her coat and was leaning against Arielle's locker, waiting. Judging by the look on her friend's face, Arielle could tell she was still angry.

"Please don't keep asking, Liz. I won't show you the pendant."

"Rose wants to see it, too."

"Liz, I can't."

"Says who?"

"The woman."

"So this woman tells you to do something, and you do it?"

"She told me to keep it hidden, so that's what I'm going to do. Now move over so I can get my stuff or we're going to miss the bus."

Elizabeth stared at the other girl for a second before stepping aside. Arielle stashed textbooks into her bag and pulled on her coat. The two girls hurried down the hallway leading to the schoolyard where the row of yellow buses waited. As they stepped outside, Elizabeth nudged her friend with her elbow. Arielle looked up and spotted Simon Vanesse and Lea Darling less than an arm's length away, kissing passionately. Lea *Dahling* (as Arielle and Elizabeth called her behind her back) opened her eyes for a moment and noticed Arielle staring at her. She grabbed Arielle's arm as she walked past.

"What are *you* looking at, Pumpkin?"

Lea rarely spoke to Arielle—it was as if she thought Arielle were contagious or something—but when she did, she always called her Pumpkin.

Arielle lowered her gaze. She wished she had the courage to say, "Hey, chill out, *Dahling*," but she couldn't bring herself to speak the words.

Lea's mouth curled into a malicious grin when she realized why Arielle was so uncomfortable.

"You want to get with my boyfriend, don't you?"

A rush of hot shame turned Arielle's cheeks scarlet. Disarmed by Lea's accurate, though tactless, observation, the chubby teenager stood there—frustratingly helpless—as her face, blazing like a neon sign, laid bare her innermost desire.

"Relax, Lea," said Simon. "She didn't do anything."

Had Arielle heard correctly? Had Simon just come to her rescue? She had been so shaken by Lea's hostility, she had almost forgotten: this wasn't the first time Simon ever defended her.

When they were in elementary school, Simon had prevented that big lug Richard from making fun of her in front of the entire class. Elizabeth never tired of hearing that story; in fact, she kept badgering Arielle to tell it again.

During gym class in the fall one year, the teacher had decided that the students would play dodgeball outside. He named Simon and Richard team captains. The two boys took turns picking their teams, and it looked like Arielle was going to be left until last—as usual. She was now the only student left, and it was Richard's turn to pick. Standing with her back against the wall of the school, she waited for him to say her name. Instead of calling her over to join his team, Richard slowly walked towards her. Arielle could still recall his cruel sneer. "You can have her!" he shouted. What he really meant was:

she's so useless that we don't want her on our team. Anyone who is always picked last knows he (or she) is the least popular student in gym class, so having one's nose rubbed in it makes the rejection twice as humiliating. And for Arielle, the dreadful feeling of shame that washed over her was, unfortunately, a familiar one.

"Richard, leave her alone!" Someone had yelled from the crowd of students. It was Simon's voice, she was sure of it!

Richard froze, his beady eyes opening as wide as they could get. It was now *his* turn to feel uncomfortable. No-one, not even the big kids in grade 6, dared challenge Simon Vanesse. Even back then, Simon was the most popular and respected student at school. Without a word, Richard meekly returned to his team, shoulders slumped in defeat. Simon's face-saving move may have only been cosmetic, but Arielle had been thrilled nonetheless.

BACK IN THE schoolyard of Glory High, Arielle raised her head, and her and Simon's eyes locked for a second. *Ms. Dahling* whirled around to glare at her boyfriend.

"What's wrong with you? Why are you sticking up for this loser?"

Lea was angry. *Perfect*, thought Arielle. *Maybe now he'll realize that she's not right for him and that he deserves someone better. Like me!*

"C'mon, Lea," Simon replied. "It's no big deal."

The students gathered nearby, who had been watching in silence, were glad to not be in Arielle's shoes.

"This isn't over, Pumpkin!" Lea spat out the words before releasing Arielle's arm and waving her impatiently away. Simon and Lea then returned to their embrace. Arielle fought the urge to apologize for having bothered them. Messing in the lives of VanLea was like dissing

Hollywood's biggest power couple—and all their fans. Simon and Lea were the two most popular students in school. Every guy wanted to be like Simon, and every girl, like Lea. Many were prepared to sacrifice their old friendships for the opportunity to hang out with them.

"Why didn't you say something?" Elizabeth asked Arielle as they rushed towards the bus.

"Say what, exactly?"

"Just put her in her place!"

Arielle shook her head. "Liz, Lea is Simon's *girlfriend*."

"And your point is?"

They were approaching the bus as the door started to close. Arielle waved at the driver to get his attention, but he didn't notice.

"He's going to leave without us!" she exclaimed.

Elizabeth looked on in dismay.

"Hang on!" someone yelled from behind them. A boy sprinted by to their right. He reached the bus first and pounded on the door.

"WAIT!" he bellowed.

The door opened, but the boy did not board. Arielle had recognized him by his long hair flapping in the wind as he ran past: it was the new student, the one who had tussled with Simon and his friends in the cafeteria.

"After you, ladies," he said with a bow.

He was clearly pleased to have been of service. A long, brown coat hung open from his broad shoulders, revealing a black turtleneck sweater. He wore grey construction boots. On each wrist was a wide leather bracelet decorated with an owl made of metal studs. Although grateful for his help, Arielle thought he was much too cocky.

The two girls thanked him and got on the bus. He followed them and chose the seat directly behind theirs.

"I'm Emmanuel Bolinger," he said, introducing

himself.

"Are you new?" Elizabeth asked as she turned to face him.

"Is it that obvious?"

"Where did you live before?"

"In the city."

"Why did you move to Glory?"

"I had to switch schools, so my grandmother decided to come here."

Elizabeth glanced at Arielle, a twinkle in her eye.

"Why did you *have* to switch schools?"

Emmanuel leaned forward and whispered, "Because demons tried to kill me."

Chapter 3

Elizabeth froze…

And her eyes, already magnified by her glasses, grew even larger.

"Oh…Really? That's—uh—that's a very good reason for switching schools," she stammered.

The conversation came to a halt, crushed beneath the anvil of Emmanuel's remark. Out of the corner of her eye, Arielle saw the long-haired boy smile. He seemed to think making fun of her friend was funny. She didn't share his sense of humour.

He got off the bus two stops before theirs.

"What was that all about?" Elizabeth asked, watching him through the window as the bus pulled away from the curb.

"It's his idea of a joke. He's just playing with your head."

"Maybe he likes to live dangerously."

"Demons, Liz? Get real!"

Elizabeth hesitated before adding, "He's kind of cute."

Arielle's first reaction was to tell Liz that he wasn't her type, but realized her best friend had a point: Emmanuel *did* have a certain appeal after all. His long hair, the swagger in his grin and his unconventional sense of style made him look deliciously rebellious…

"He is, kind of," Arielle agreed, mainly for her friend's benefit.

Elizabeth smiled as her eyes lit up. *Here we go again,* Arielle thought. *Some guy talks to her for three seconds, and she falls in love!*

BRUTUS meowed his usual greeting to his owner before returning to his daily routine, which, as far as Arielle could tell, consisted of eating and sleeping.

Arielle crossed the living room to the kitchen.

"Hi, Uncle Yvan," she said as she set her bag down on the table.

Her uncle was a pharmacist and owned a small drug store downtown. Business was doing well, so they never went without.

He nodded in greeting. Arielle noticed the open bottle of wine before him on the counter. He had already started drinking.

No-one looking at Uncle Yvan could tell he was an alcoholic. Tall and thin, he seemed to be in perfect health. His classic haircut and neatly trimmed beard boosted his professional image and that, along with his serious and reserved manner, were interpreted as signs of worldly experience. Only Arielle and Elizabeth knew about his drinking problem.

"Did you have a good day?" Arielle asked politely.

Uncle Yvan's response: a shrug.

"I have a lot of homework. I better get started right away."

"Juliette came by earlier," her uncle said. "She made macaroni casserole. It's in the fridge."

He filled his wine glass and left the room. Arielle

heard him walk into the living room and turn the TV on.

Juliette came by twice a week to do the housework and prepare their meals. Uncle Yvan hated cooking. It was a good thing, too, because he was definitely no master chef. The last time he tried to make chicken was a total disaster.

Arielle opened her bag and removed the novel her English teacher had asked the class to read by next month: *Dr. Jekyll and Mr. Hyde*. Just then, Arielle heard the voice of the woman from the video in her mind, *"Don't forget. You have to fall asleep before sundown."*

The teenager heated some macaroni in the microwave and took it up to her room, where she planned to do her homework. Elizabeth called a little after five.

"Did you change your mind? I can still come over if you want."

"No, that's OK, Liz," Arielle replied.

"Will you be able to fall asleep so early?"

"I don't know, actually. My uncle's got some sleeping pills in his room. Maybe I could take one."

"Oh, Elle, don't do that! My dad says those pills can turn you into a drug addict."

"Liz, your dad is a beekeeper. What does he know about sleeping pills?"

"Well, he knows more than you."

A sigh escaped Arielle's lips. "OK, I won't take any sleeping pills then. Happy?"

"Yes."

Arielle promised Elizabeth she would call her at the first sign of trouble, and then the girls hung up. Brutus came to lie by her feet and began to purr. Arielle managed to read a few pages of her homework assignment before she fell asleep. She hadn't needed the sleeping pill after all.

"Arielle? Arielle, can you hear me?"

Someone was talking to her in her sleep.

"You're not dreaming, Arielle, I'm real."

The teenager's eyelids felt heavy—her entire *body* felt heavy. Arielle forced herself to open her eyes. According to her alarm clock, it was 9:23 p.m.

"Are you the woman I spoke to this morning?" asked Arielle. She actually *thought* the question rather than spoke it out loud.

"Yes."

"Where are you?"

"Inside you."

"Inside me?"

"The pendant you're wearing lets me speak to you."

Arielle felt it grow warm against her flesh. The voice spoke again.

"I could have used it to talk to you this morning, but I thought it might scare you. That's why I set up your uncle's video camera instead."

"And you think speaking to me like this isn't scaring me?"

"I thought you would have figured out who I am by now."

"No, I haven't. Who are you, anyway?"

There was a pause.

"I am you, Arielle…"

Chapter 4

"You—you're me?"

Arielle felt this couldn't possibly be true—unless she was losing her mind.

"*Another version of you,*" added the voice.

"I must be dreaming."

Arielle sat up and fumbled for the phone.

"*Arielle, calm down.*"

"Where's the damn phone?"

"*You want to call Elizabeth? It's not as if she can do anything to help you.*"

"We'll see about that..."

"Looking for something?" A third voice chimed in—and this one was not in her head. Someone else was in the room!

The light turned on. Once Arielle's eyes adjusted to the brightness, she noticed an enormous, hairy beast in the corner. The creature was sitting on a chair, holding the telephone in its paws. Arielle's shriek was pure terror.

"Calm down, Arielle. It's just me."

Surprisingly, the creature spoke in a normal-sounding voice and not in the monstrous snarl she was expecting.

"Don't you recognize me?"

Huddled beneath the covers, Arielle studied the beast

carefully. It appeared to be a tiger with white whiskers, but was wearing human clothes and boots. The fur on its face was a patchwork of grey and white. But there was something about the notch in the creature's left ear that seemed familiar…

Then Arielle remembered that Brutus' left ear was notched in about the same place.

"*It's him, all right,*" said the voice in her mind.

"Huh?" said Arielle.

The creature tilted its head.

"What's the matter, cat got your tongue?"

Arielle couldn't believe her eyes.

"Brutus?!?"

He nodded, and then burst out laughing.

"You should see the look on your face, Mistress!"

Arielle was flabbergasted, wondering how else she should look upon learning that not only could her cat change into human form, he could speak, too!

"*Let me explain,*" said the woman's voice. "*Brutus is an Animalter. At night, he takes human form to better serve the Alter who is his master.*"

"I don't understand," said Arielle, still trembling from shock. "What's an Alter?"

"*Have you ever heard of multiple personality disorder?*"

"In a movie, I think, once."

"*'Alter' is a word that refers to each personality of someone with multiple personalities.*"

"Are you saying I'm crazy?"

"*No, you're not. This is a different type of Alter.*"

"And I suppose that makes you my 'Alter'."

"*Yes, I live inside you, Arielle. I can do whatever I want after you fall asleep. Your mind rests when I take control of your body, which is why you're never tired in the morning— and why you can't remember what I was doing with your body the night before.*"

"So you control my body at night?"

"You live during the day, and I live at night. But all that's about to change. Now that you have the pendant, you can speak to me and stay in control of your body at all times."

"What's your name?"

"Elleira: it's Arielle spelled backwards. That is how we Alters distinguish ourselves from Dayforms."

"Are there any more like you?"

"Many, many more. And you will meet them tonight, if you still want to help me."

"What do I have to do?"

"Just one thing: go to Simon Vanesse's house. His Alter, Nomis, is throwing a party tonight. We have to be there."

"Simon Vanesse has an Alter, too?"

"He's not the only person you know who has one."

Now he and I have one thing in common, thought Arielle.

"Why do I have to go to his party?"

"I can't explain yet."

Arielle mulled this request over. All she would have to do is show up at a party—*Simon's* party.

"Keep away from Nomis," warned Elleira.

Arielle had forgotten that her Alter could hear her thoughts.

"Is he dangerous?"

"Just go to the party, and I'll handle the rest. You'll get control of your body back by tomorrow morning, I promise. Tonight will be the last time I take over. I'm fading, Arielle."

"What are you trying to tell me?"

Elleira hesitated.

"I am going to die before sunrise."

CHAPTER 5

"Get up now."

Arielle obeyed and climbed out of bed. Brutus was still comfortably sprawled on the chair. He winked at her conspiratorially, his Cheshire grin reassuring her that he was, indeed, who he claimed to be. Arielle eyed him suspiciously.

Elleira had told her to stand in front of the mirror with her hand on the pendant.

"There are two copies of this pendant. Each one allows the person wearing it to stay in control of their body when in their Alter form. At dawn, you will change back to your Dayform, even if you're wearing the pendant."

Alter form? Arielle had no idea what Elleira was talking about.

"You'll see in a minute. Just say the words written on the pendant."

Arielle studied the inscription and read the words out loud, "Fra Retla! Fra Alter!"

The transformation started at once. She watched in amazement as her curly hair slowly straightened out, each lock unwinding and taking on a darker hue.

"What's happening?!"

"*You're turning into me,*" replied Elleira calmly.

Intense pain shot through the muscles of Arielle's arms and legs, like they were being used in a tug-of-war; she felt they would snap if it didn't stop. Her steadily lengthening—and now jet-black—hair had reached her shoulders. She grew several inches taller, and her freckles faded. Her pyjama top grew snug around her more defined bosom.

"*How do you like your new look?*"

Arielle blinked a few times as she stared at her reflection. She saw an image of a tall and slender young woman with a flawless complexion. Her hair was straight and black.

"So this is why I thought you looked like me," Arielle said as she recognized the woman from the video.

"*You're not done. You have to change your clothes.*"

Elleira steered Arielle to the closet.

"*There is a hidden compartment at the back. To open it, press the yellow butterfly.*"

The back of the closet was covered with flowered wallpaper.

"What butterfly? All I see are flowers."

"*Look down and to the right,*" said Elleira. "*You should see a butterfly that looks like the birthmark on your shoulder.*"

Arielle rolled up her sleeve and examined her birthmark. She had never realized it before, but it *did* look like a butterfly. She returned her attention to the wallpaper and finally spotted the image of the winged insect where her Alter said it would be. The image was identical to her peculiar birthmark.

Arielle reached out and gently pushed the image with her finger. A panel slid back, revealing a second closet behind the first. Inside were hung three sets of clothing, each consisting of a pair of pants, a blouse, a long leather coat and a pair of boots.

"*These are your clothes now. Go on, get dressed.*"

Arielle grabbed one of the outfits, exposing a small niche in the far wall filled with small, silver cylinders.

"What are those?"

"*I'll explain later,*" answered Elleira. "*Now hurry, it's getting late. We have to go.*"

Arielle quickly slipped on her new clothes and turned to admire her reflection.

"Rooowwrrrrr!" growled Brutus throatily from the other side of the room. "Catwoman never looked so good!"

Brutus was right: she was gorgeous. The outfit flattered Arielle's figure. Never in her life had she felt so beautiful, so desirable.

"Tonight, I have become what I have always dreamed of being," she said as tears welled up in her eyes.

"*And a whole lot more, believe me,*" added Elleira. "*So, do you still want to help me?*"

"Will it be dangerous?"

"*Not if you do as I say.*"

"All right, I'll help you."

Arielle trusted her Alter, but that was not the reason she agreed to her request. She was definitely *not* going to pass up the opportunity to show up at Simon's party with the body of a goddess.

Brutus rose and walked towards Arielle.

"Let's get going, Mistress."

"Wait! What happens if my uncle decides to check in on me? He'll expect to find me asleep in bed."

"There's no chance of that happening," replied Brutus. "He just finished off a whole bottle of whiskey. He'll be out until morning."

Chapter 6

They crept downstairs and crossed from the living room to the kitchen.

Uncle Yvan was splayed across the sofa, fast asleep. Arielle and Brutus exited through the kitchen door, which led into the back yard. Although it was a cool night, Arielle, curiously, did not feel the chill. She glanced at her watch: it was nearly 10 p.m.

"*We have to get to Bombyx Manor,*" said Elleira. "*The sun will rise at about 6:30 a.m. We have a little more than eight hours.*"

"Bombyx Manor is near Crooked Lake," gasped Arielle. "That's way on the other side of town!"

"Watch and learn, Mistress," Brutus said. He gripped the two ends of his coat and thrust them back. A wind started blowing about him, causing his coat to snap sharply. Slowly, Brutus began to rise until he was hovering six feet in the air. Arielle craned her head back to follow his upward movement.

"We can be there in less than ten minutes," he assured her.

"How did you *do* that?"

"We are creatures of the night, Arielle. The moon is our mother—she watches over us and protects us. She is the source of all our special powers. Now, you try!"

Arielle grabbed the ends of her coat as Brutus had done. Instantly, wind began swirling about her, piercing through her clothing and brushing against her skin. The teenager suddenly felt as light as a feather. As she slowly rose, she had to extend the tips of her toes downward to stay in contact with the ground.

"Whoa!" she exclaimed nervously.

"It's all right, Arielle," said Brutus. "You're doing great."

Arielle closed her eyes and focused on remaining calm. Her coat bulged under the onrush of air, and she began to lift up once more. She soon found herself dangling in mid-air, her legs swinging back and forth. She flew up next to Brutus, but unable to stabilize herself, she continued to float upwards. Arielle felt her Animalter grab her with a paw and slowly pull her towards him.

"Things starting to look up?" he asked when they were face-to-face.

"You could say that," she answered, laughing.

Brutus grinned. Arielle wondered if she would ever get used to seeing her cat make such human expressions.

"Flying is like swimming," explained Brutus. "You know how to swim, right?"

Arielle nodded.

"When you swim, you have to move your arms and legs to propel yourself through the water."

Arielle nodded again.

"The same principle applies to flying, except you don't use your arms and legs to move forward, you use your mind. Just think of a direction and that's where you'll go."

Arielle took a deep breath to settle the butterflies in

her stomach. She pictured herself in the middle of a lake. To hover, she found that all she had to do was imagine she was treading water.

"There," said Brutus, releasing his grip.

Arielle drifted upwards once more, but managed to return to her original position without too much trouble. She was now flying above her neighbourhood, she realized, really and truly *flying*. The very idea left her giddy and excited.

Brutus congratulated her on her progress and indicated it was time for her second lesson. He brought his legs together and held his arms over his head.

"The best way to fly is the 'superhero position'," he said matter-of-factly as he tilted his body forward until he was parallel to the ground "It's more aerodynamic— and cuts down on the risk of hitting a bird."

As Arielle copied Brutus, she noticed that her Alter form was more graceful, and considerably more agile, than her human form.

"Follow me," said Brutus, speeding into the night.

Arielle focused her thoughts and set off, quickly catching up to the Animalter. They were flying so fast the wind whistled in their ears, yet she barely felt the cold on her exposed skin. The two of them cut through the air like a pair of arrows fired at the same target.

THE residential neighbourhoods below gave way to the business district. Arielle and Brutus veered towards downtown and continued in the direction of the Silver Slopes ski resort, where most of the hotels in the region were clustered. They bypassed the mountain on its western flank and headed for the forest to the north.

"There!" yelled Brutus, pointing to a large clearing.

Arielle spotted Crooked Lake. A number of lights twinkling through the trees near the shore revealed the location of Bombyx Manor.

"Be careful when you land," cautioned Brutus. "Keep your legs limber—pretend they're springs."

Arielle nodded, and the two of them began their descent. As they approached the manor, she saw that Brutus was now flying feet first and holding his arms over his head, like a parachutist about to land. Twisting clumsily in mid-air, she copied his position. Brutus gave her a thumbs-up, and then pointed to a grove below. She nodded in acknowledgement. She watched the Animalter touch down smoothly.

Unfortunately, her own landing did not go quite as well.

The trees grew larger at a frightening rate as Arielle approached the ground. She was coming in too fast! Brutus frantically waved his arms. Too late! She shut her eyes and braced for impact. This was going to hurt.

The next few seconds were chaotic. Arielle heard branches snap as she barrelled through the treetops. Images of her impending doom flashed through her mind: she would smash into the ground, breaking every bone in her body. If she survived, she would probably be completely paralyzed and spend the rest of her life in a wheelchair.

It took her a few moments to realize that her freefall had ended painlessly. Arielle had the impression she was floating.

I must have broken my spine—no wonder I don't feel anything! She thought, resigning herself to her fate.

"*It takes a lot more than a little fall to hurt an Alter,*" said Elleira.

"A *little* fall?!?" Arielle considered her landing to be more of the meteor-smashing-into-the-Earth variety. She slowly opened her eyes and saw Brutus studying her with a look of concern. He was holding her in his arms.

At the last second, he had leaped up and caught her.

"You really need to work on your landings," he said.

She nodded, overjoyed at being alive—and unhurt. Brutus set her down and brushed off her coat with his paw.

"Do you like flying?" he asked.

"Yeah, except for the last part," she replied.

"Not bad for your inaugural flight."

"You're too kind."

The Animalter led her to a spot from where they could watch the manor in secret. Several cars were parked in the esplanade near the foot of the sweeping marble staircase leading to a terrace, at the far end of which was the main entrance.

"Some Alters prefer more traditional means of transportation," whispered Brutus, pointing towards the cars.

A pair of dog-headed men was standing watch by the front door. They looked like two-legged Dobermans and were dressed similarly to Arielle and Brutus.

"Dog Animalters. I *hate* dog Animalters," grumbled Brutus.

Arielle kept staring at the two were-dogs.

"Can other types of animals be Animalters?"

Brutus turned to Arielle, a gleam in his eye.

"How do you think parrots learned to talk?"

The manor door opened. A young man came out and began talking to the two DoberMen. Arielle recognized the scar on his cheek: the young man was Noah Davidoff. As she studied his face, she noticed this version of Noah was much different from the boy she knew from school. He was taller and had a harder set to his features. He looked older than his sixteen years.

"That's Razan, Noah's Alter," said Brutus.

"Razan? But that isn't Noah spelled backwards,"

Arielle pointed out.

"*Noah's real name is Nazar Ivanovitch Davidoff,*" Elleira explained. "*It's a Russian name. And Nazar spelled backwards is Razan.*"

"Why would he change his first name?" asked Arielle.

"Noah is a childhood nickname," said Brutus. "He thought by using it he wouldn't stand out as much and that he would be more popular with girls." Brutus rolled his eyes and scoffed.

Noah's Alter turned his head and looked directly at where Arielle and Brutus were hiding.

"He heard us," Brutus lowered his voice.

Arielle studied Noah's face, recalling the lunchtime incident in the cafeteria.

"He knows I have the pendant," Arielle whispered frantically.

"*That's true,*" said Elleira.

"Could it be a problem?"

"*Not if everything goes as planned.*"

CHAPTER 7

Brutus crept out of their hiding place and held out his paw to Arielle. She hesitated to take it.

"What happens if they find out I'm not Elleira?" she asked.

"Everything will be fine. Don't worry about it," assured Brutus.

Arielle took her Animalter's paw, and the two of them walked towards the manor.

Elleira outlined her plan to Arielle.

"I will take control of your body once we're inside the manor. There's something I have to do. But I won't be in control for very long—only a few minutes. I'm so weak..."

"Will I know what you'll be doing?"

"No. When I'm done, you'll just think you fell asleep."

Arielle and Brutus climbed the stairs, shoulder to shoulder. Arielle was nervous. Clenching her hands, she noticed they were clammy. She fought to calm herself, since it was important she not let on that anything was out of the ordinary. She had a hunch that the other

Alters wouldn't hesitate to hurt her if they learned she wasn't one of them.

"*Everything is going to be OK,*" Elleira reassured the frightened girl.

Razan did not take his eyes off them from the moment they stepped out of the woods. Arielle decided that he was broader—and much more handsome—than the Noah she saw every day at school. His dark clothing and no-nonsense manner made him appear more mature. A sword hung from his waist, and a number of silver cylinders similar to the ones in her closet were attached in a row to his belt. What purpose could they possibly serve?

The two DoberMen blocked their passage to the main entrance.

"Well, if it isn't Garfield," snarked one of the dog-headed men.

"Shut up, Odie, or I'll dump your food bowl on your head," retorted Brutus.

"What were you doing over there?" asked Razan, pointing towards the woods.

"Trouble with the landing gear," said Brutus.

Suspicious, Noah's Alter held them in his steely glare for a few moments, and then stepped aside.

"Let them pass," he ordered.

The two DoberMen obeyed immediately.

"What a couple of well-trained mutts!" exclaimed Brutus in mock admiration. "If you sit up and beg, I'll give you a doggie treat."

"Get stuffed, Nermal," growled one of the dogs as it opened the front door.

Razan led Arielle and Brutus into the manor. Techno music could be heard as they walked down the entry hall, growing louder as they approached the room that seemed to be their destination. Arielle could feel the floor vibrate to the pounding rhythm.

"The party's going to be in the ballroom," yelled Brutus to make himself heard over the din.

Another Animalter, this one with a raven's head, stood guard at a pair of double doors. As the trio drew near, he bowed his head in greeting. Razan gestured for the man-raven to open the doors. The Animalter leaped to obey.

No longer dampened by any barrier, the music burst forth, striking them like a physical force. The ballroom was packed with young people dancing wildly, their shadowy forms bathed in a bluish light originating from the four corners of the room. They were all dressed in black clothing, and each had a leather coat identical to the ones worn by Arielle and Brutus. In the dim light, their faces seemed to have a phosphorescent glow, and their coats appeared to move like an extension of their bodies.

"*These are Alters,*" said Elleira.

Glancing around the room, Arielle recognized many of the faces.

"*Don't forget that these people are nothing like the ones you see every day, even if they look a lot alike,*" cautioned Elleira.

Arielle and Brutus followed Razan as he crossed the room. The dancing figures stepped aside to let them pass without breaking their rhythm. Many of the other Alters looked longingly at Arielle, but she did not notice. The three of them had almost reached the far wall when the music stopped. All eyes turned to the trio. Razan opened his mouth to speak, but reconsidered and said nothing.

A spotlight clicked on, and the beam did a zigzag sweep of the crowd before settling on the five figures standing on a stage in the centre of the room. One of them was holding a microphone and looking at Arielle.

"Let's all give a warm welcome to Elleira, our very own—and very lovely—Venus!"

Arielle would recognize that voice anywhere.

"*Altermorphosis does not change your voice,*" explained Elleira. "*You may think that's Simon Vanesse up there with the microphone, but it isn't. That's actually Nomis, his Alter. Be careful around him. He's very dangerous.*"

Arielle studied Nomis carefully. Elleira was right; the Simon she was in love with was very different from his Alter on stage.

"Come up here, Venus!" Nomis waved for her to join him.

"Why does he keep calling me Venus?" Arielle asked Elleira.

"*The Elders claim that they have never seen an Alter as beautiful as me,*" said Elleira. "*Look around you. The boys all want you, and the girls are all jealous of you.*"

Sure enough, Arielle could see the desire and envy in the eyes fixed upon her. Having never been the object of such attention, she felt flattered—and rather intimidated.

"*This is your Alter body now. It is up to you to take care of it,*" added Elleira.

No problem there, Arielle thought with satisfaction. Now she knew how the ugly duckling felt when it turned into a lovely swan.

"Come join us!" Nomis repeated from the stage.

The speakers amplified his already powerful voice, making his request sound like a command. The four other figures drew closer to him. They were the Alters of Lea Darling and the CeeCees. In their Alter forms, the four young women were even more attractive than their Dayforms, but none of them were as stunning as Arielle. For once, much to her surprise, Arielle was the most beautiful girl in the room!

The crowd began clapping and chanting Elleira's

name. Razan did not take his eyes off Arielle. He seemed to be waiting for her to react. Arielle turned to Brutus, who shook his head. The Alters increased their clamour as they pressed around Arielle. She felt caught in a vise.

The sound of an explosion silenced the crowd. The Alters exchanged anxious glances.

"What's going on?" Arielle whispered to Brutus. He did not answer. She noticed that his ears were twitching furiously as they sought a clue to this mysterious interruption. Suddenly, an Alter burst into the room through the double doors, a look of terror on his face.

"The Sylphors! The Sylphors are here!" he shrieked.

"*The Dark Elves are attacking!*" exclaimed Elleira.

"Elves? Are you kidding me?" Arielle blurted out.

The Alters scattered in a panic.

"*Hurry! Take off the pendant!*" ordered Elleira. "*I need to take control of your body!*"

Arielle pretended to stumble, quickly removing the pendant as Brutus reached out to steady her. She was instantly aware of another presence in her mind, and that presence was growing. Within seconds, Arielle could neither speak nor move, effectively becoming a spectator in a body whose limbs she could not control. She could only watch as the Alters ran helter-skelter around the room.

"*Close your eyes and sleep,*" said Elleira.

All of the windows in the ballroom shattered with a terrible crash. Several shadowy figures entered the room through the windows, some leaping over the sills, others flying overhead.

In the midst of the chaos, Arielle went limp, like she had been drugged. Although she fought to stay awake, the Alters' cries gradually grew fainter. The last thing she was aware of was a man's voice yelling, "Over here, quick!"

CHAPTER 8

"*Too weak,*" said a voice inside her head.

The haze slowly cleared from Arielle's mind. As she gradually regained control of her body, the blackness of a deep sleep was replaced by that of the night sky.

"*Too weak to fly.*"

Arielle felt the blood begin to flow in her veins, like sap in a tree after the spring thaw. She realized she had been running all this time, plunging through a forest, branches whipping at her face and clothes. Though she was breathing heavily and her legs ached, she did not slow down. The tiny bit of moonlight peeking through the clouds was her only source of illumination. She could make out no trail as she fled—from what? She paused to look at her watch: 11:05 p.m. She had been unconscious for about fifteen minutes. What had happened?

"Run, Arielle! Run!" called a voice from behind her.

She felt something cold on her chest. The pendant was once again hanging from around her neck. Was Elleira still alive inside her? One thing was certain: Arielle could no longer feel her Alter's presence. She was all alone in a body that seemed too big for her.

She heard barking—Razan must be using the DoberMen Animalters to track her! Arielle guessed they had taken on their animal form to follow her scent. If that were the case, she felt it was pointless to try to escape. Even in her Alter body, she could not outrun a dog. To make matters worse, she did not have the strength to fly away.

"Arielle!" yelled a voice directly behind her. "There's a path to the right. Take it!"

A shadow bore down upon her as she glanced over her shoulder. In the moonlight, she could make out a face: it was Emmanuel Bolinger, the new student.

"Don't stop! Keep running!" he said as he grabbed her arm and dragged her towards a faint trail through the woods.

"Come on. The road isn't far."

Arielle could hear the barking grow louder and louder. She suddenly felt the strength flow into her limbs and her senses grow keener. She increased her speed and was soon outpacing Emmanuel, who was struggling to maintain his grip on her arm. Now she was grabbing *him* so that he could keep up with *her*.

"Hurry, they're catching up!" she said.

They sprinted all the way to Gleason Road, which led from Crooked Lake and Bombyx Manor all the way back to town.

"There!" said Emmanuel, pointing to an old Chevrolet parked on the shoulder of the road. They ran to the vehicle.

"This is my grandmother's car," he explained, pulling the keys out of his pocket.

"The dogs!" Arielle shouted as she spotted the two Dobermans bounding out of the woods in animal form, one after the other.

The two teenagers got into the car and slammed the doors—and not a moment too soon! Barking furiously, the dogs hurled themselves against the side of the car and leaped at the windows, draping the vehicle with their frothy saliva. The whole scene was unnerving. Arielle felt the dogs would do anything to get at them, going as far as ripping the car apart with their teeth.

Emmanuel turned the key in the ignition. The engine caught for a second, then sputtered and died. He swore. Arielle turned to Emmanuel, who was repeatedly, though unsuccessfully, attempting to start the car.

"Hurry!" she urged

"I'm trying!"

Arielle heard a curious whistling coming from outside. Glancing upward through the windshield, she spotted a dark shape fly overhead. It circled the car before landing heavily on the hood. The vehicle rocked under the impact.

"What was that?" she gasped.

"An Alter," Emmanuel replied grimly.

The shape rose gracefully. Arielle recognized the scarred face staring impassively back at her: it was Razan, the Alter of Noah Davidoff.

Razan was now standing on the hood, the edge of his coat flapping as if blown by a strong wind. He reached for the sword he wore at his belt and drew it in one swift motion.

"That's a draugur blade," screamed Emmanuel, shrinking back into his seat.

Razan pointed his glowing weapon at the other boy and walked towards him, the hood groaning under every step.

"He's going to kill us!" Emmanuel was panicking. "Draugur blades can cut through anything!"

Suddenly, the blade became nearly transparent, like a ghost. Razan lunged forward, thrusting his weapon through the windshield. Emmanuel managed to duck as the sword stabbed into the headrest. Peeking over the dashboard, Emmanuel turned the keys in the ignition once more. This time, the engine revved.

"Go!" shrieked Arielle. The teenaged boy slammed on the gas. The Chevrolet jumped forward, causing Razan to lose his balance. He tumbled over the roof of the car, bounced off the trunk and landed in a heap on the pavement.

"We did it!" crowed Emmanuel as he floored the pedal. The car raced down Gleason Road. Looking out the rear window, Arielle saw Razan climb to his feet. The Alter simply stood and watched the car vanish into the night. Barking madly, the Dobermans instantly gave chase, but the speeding vehicle left them in the dust. Arielle sighed with relief.

The sword was still sticking through the windshield, which, strangely enough, was not even cracked. The eerie blade formed a wall between driver and passenger. After a few minutes, Emmanuel stopped the car and got out. Grabbing the pommel of the draugur sword, he pulled it gently out of the windshield before laying it carefully on the back seat.

"That'll come in handy," he said as he slipped behind the wheel.

"What are you going to do with it?" asked Arielle, puzzled at why he would ever need a *sword*, of all things.

Emmanuel looked at the girl and grinned.

"I'm going to use it to wipe every Alter off the face of the Earth."

Chapter 9

They drove for several minutes in awkward silence.

Arielle decided to speak when she could see the lights of the town in the distance.

"What were you doing at the manor, Emmanuel?"

"What were *you* doing there?" the young man replied.

"I asked you first," insisted Arielle.

Emmanuel shrugged. "Reconnaissance," he said.

"Reconnaissance?!"

"I was spying," he confessed. "You have to know your enemies."

"Since when are the Alters your enemies?" she asked.

"Ever since they killed my parents," he spat out the words.

Arielle did not know what to say. Elleira had never mentioned that Alters kill people, but after seeing Razan and his two DoberMen in action, she had no doubt about their capacity for violence.

"Sylphors and Alters have been at war for centuries," explained Emmanuel. "Sometimes humans get caught in the crossfire. That's what happened to my parents: they were innocent bystanders who were in the wrong place at the wrong time—like the two of us tonight."

"I'm sorry, Emmanuel," said Arielle with genuine sympathy. "My parents died, too. In a fire. I was just a baby when it happened."

"Then we have something in common," said Emmanuel. "We're both orphans."

"Is that why you live with your grandmother?" asked the young girl.

"Yeah. Her name is Saddington. She's the one who is showing me how to fight Alters."

"*Fight* Alters? Are you serious?"

"Yeah, I fight them. I've still got a few tricks left to learn, but one day, I'll be a full-fledged 'Alter hunter'. And the Alters in this town will be my first prey."

Arielle eyed him nervously.

"Are you going to hunt me, too?"

"No, you're not an Alter."

"Why do you say that?"

"Your pendant," he answered. "Whoever wears it can control his—or her—Alter. That's how I knew you weren't one of *them* when I saw you running earlier."

Arielle put her hand to her neck. A couple of the buttons on her blouse were undone, leaving the pendant exposed. She kicked herself for not noticing sooner. How long had the pendant been visible?

"Don't worry," said Emmanuel reassuringly. "I won't tell anyone."

Arielle's mind was reeling. "Are you the one who helped me to escape from the manor?"

"I'd have liked to, but no, it wasn't me."

"Do you know what happened, then?" she asked.

"I was hiding in the woods, watching. After the Elves attacked, I saw you run outside. Before you disappeared into the woods, I saw the pendant around your neck. A few seconds later, the two Doberman Animalters appeared on the terrace. They changed into their dog form and took off after you. It was obvious they were hunting you, so I thought that you might need a hand."

"Was I alone?"

"Yes."

That meant Brutus hadn't been able to escape, at least not at the same time she had. Was he still back at the manor? Was he fighting Elves? Was he even *alive*? She shuddered briefly, fearing the worst, but pushed that thought aside and turned back to Emmanuel.

"Why did you call the Elves 'Sylphors'?"

"The Dark Elves call *themselves* Sylphors. They're bad news and pretty hardcore. To make themselves look different from the Light Elves—who are good—they shave their heads and act tough. Sylphors may be elves, but you sure won't find any of them working in Santa's workshop wearing pointy shoes and jingly hats."

Emmanuel glanced at the young woman.

"OK, now it's your turn. Why were *you* at the manor?"

"My Alter wanted me to go, so I did. She told me she was dying and that there was one last thing she wanted to do," Arielle replied.

"Dying? That can only mean she was in love with someone."

Sensing Arielle's confusion, Emmanuel explained that while Alters are powerful demons, they have one major weakness: love. They are so twisted, affection is like poison to them. If an Alter falls in love, his soul begins to weaken, and he will die within a couple of nights.

"And that must be why Elleira revealed herself to you. She wasn't strong enough to control your body anymore. That little trip to the manor must have been pretty important to her."

Arielle grew worried.

"Will I die, too?"

Emmanuel shook his head.

"When an Alter dies because it falls in love, the host body remains alive. The Alter spirit is the only thing that dies. Once the Alter is gone, the host returns to its human form."

"Does that mean that once Elleira dies, I won't be able to change back to my Alter body?" Arielle asked glumly. The idea of being pudgy and plain forever terrified her.

"Nope," said Emmanuel and grinned reassuringly. "If you wear the pendant, you can take the form of your Alter at night, even if your Alter is dead. Pretty sick, huh?"

He chewed his lower lip thoughtfully.

"There *is* one little problem, though: the pendant is tied to this sort of prophecy. Which means the Alters will probably try to take it from you."

"What prophecy?" Arielle grew worried again.

"You'd really have to ask my grandmother about it. She knows a lot more than me about all this stuff," said Emmanuel matter-of-factly.

He abruptly changed the subject.

"By the way, what are you doing after school?"

"My homework," Arielle said cautiously.

"Why don't you come over tomorrow to do your homework, then? I live close to your place. I could drop you off at your house afterwards. I do have my driver's licence, you know," he added proudly.

Arielle accepted his invitation, somewhat reservedly. She wasn't sure what to make of this turn of events. Was Emmanuel exaggerating the danger she was facing? She mulled it over and decided he was not. Why would he lie about a thing like that?

They did not talk again until they arrived in front of Arielle's house.

"Do you think the Alters will come after me?"

"Hard to say. They attacked Saddington and me a

month ago."

Arielle thought back to their first conversation on the school bus.

"Then what you told Elizabeth was true, the part about having to change schools because demons tried to kill you?"

"Yes. I would have been killed if Saddington hadn't saved me," he smiled at Arielle. "We're still on for tomorrow night?"

Arielle nodded and started to open the door. Emmanuel stopped her.

"Don't tell anyone about what you saw at the manor," he cautioned. "You could put several lives in danger, especially ours."

He put his hand on Arielle's. Her instinct was to yank her hand away, but she did not.

"Your Alter used you, Arielle. I think she made you go to the manor because she wanted to see her lover one last time. It was a very risky move. Alters *cannot* be trusted. I'm telling you this so they won't be able to use you again."

"I haven't known them long enough for them to have any kind of hold over me," she said.

He grinned.

"I hope that never happens."

Arielle got out of the car and crept into the house where her uncle was still asleep on the living room sofa. She went directly upstairs to her room. She undressed, carefully storing her Alter outfit in the secret closet. Sighing wistfully, she knew there was one thing left to do. Standing in front of the mirror, she grasped the pendant and said out loud, "Fra Alter! Fra Retla!"

The transformation began immediately. Arielle shrank to her regular height, her hair lightened and began to curl, her freckles re-emerged, and her buttocks and thighs expanded unflatteringly. In a matter of seconds, she went from being a top model to a dumpy sixteen-year-old. Arielle Queen, version 1.0, was back. Glumly, she turned away from her reflection. She couldn't wait until sundown the next day, when she would be able to use the pendant once more.

Arielle put on her pyjamas and climbed into bed, exhausted. Glancing at her alarm clock, she saw that she could still grab a few hours of sleep. She shut her eyes.

"*Thank you,*" whispered Elleira. "*I got to tell him goodbye.*"

Arielle sat up.

"Who? Your boyfriend?" she asked her Alter.

"*The one who freed me,*" Elleira replied faintly.

"Emmanuel was right. You used me!"

"*This is the last conversation we will ever have, Arielle. I am dying. Soon, very, very soon, you will be on your own.*"

"Why didn't you tell me about the Alters? Or the prophecy?" Arielle was furious.

The voice in her mind was silent.

"Elleira, answer me! Why are the Alters fighting the Dark Elves?" she demanded.

"*I don't have much time left. The only advice I can give you is this: be on your guard around Alters and humans. And whatever you do, stay away from Sylphors!*"

Moonlight dimly illuminated the room.

"*I'm going now,*" sighed Elleira.

"No! Wait! Not yet!" cried Arielle.

"*Thanks to you, my love may live on…*"

"Elleira, please, no!"

But it was too late, Elleira was gone. Her passing left Arielle with a feeling of emptiness, like she had lost someone dear. And there she sat, unmoving, barely breathing, alone…

A FLURRY of movement drew her attention. It was Brutus, who had bounded onto the bed and began nuzzling her hand in that insistent way of his when he wanted to be petted. She was relieved to see her cat safe and unhurt; it made Elleira's death easier to bear.

"Where were you, l'il fuzzy guy?"

Brutus meowed in reply, and then followed this up with a yawn that exposed his sharp, white teeth. He curled up by her side.

"Are you a demon, too, kitty?"

She knew full well that he could not answer. Not in his animal form, at any rate.

The young girl looked at her alarm clock. She wouldn't be able to fall asleep, as tired as she was. There were too many things going on in her mind. Arielle decided that if she couldn't get any rest, at least she could be productive, so she grabbed the novel she was supposed to read for English class. Stroking Brutus with one hand and holding the book with the other, Arielle tried to immerse herself in the tale of *Dr. Jekyll and Mr. Hyde*. Tried—and failed. After a minute or so, she placed the book back on her nightstand and lay staring at the ceiling. She could not stop thinking about Emmanuel and the way he had touched her hand.

CHAPTER 10

After her shower the next morning, Arielle went to the kitchen and poured herself a bowl of cereal.

Uncle Yvan woke up a short while later and joined his niece in the kitchen. His pale skin and the slowness of his movements spoke volumes about his current state. He clumsily plugged in the kettle and dumped two spoonfuls of instant coffee into a mug. Arielle asked him how he felt.

"Not bad," he replied without looking at her. "I have a migraine, that's all."

"You shouldn't drink so much," she said. It was the first time she had ever dared to bring this topic up with her uncle. He stopped and slowly turned towards her. Could her boldness have been a mistake? Arielle did not know how he would react.

"So you think I drink too much, do you?"

Arielle hesitated before nodding.

"I think you're right," he admitted, stroking his beard. He then resumed the task he had interrupted a half-minute ago and added two spoonfuls of sugar to the mug. Arielle knew that she had just witnessed Uncle Yvan's entire contribution to the conversation.

"I'll be home a little later this evening," she said. "I'm going to a girlfriend's house to do my homework."

Arielle felt it unnecessary (and safer) that she not tell him she would actually be going to a *boy's* house.

"Will you be back in time for supper?"

"That depends, will you be doing the cooking?" she said, laughing.

ELIZABETH peppered Arielle with questions from the moment they met at the bus stop and did not let up even after they had boarded the bus. Emmanuel had suggested Arielle not tell anyone about their little adventure the night before. Since she did not want to put her friends' lives in danger, that was exactly what she intended to do. Arielle gave the same answer throughout Liz's interrogation, "Nothing happened last night, and I had had a nightmare the night before."

However, she was pretty sure that Liz would never buy her story.

"Are you telling me that you dreamt the whole thing up: the woman, the pendant and the video?" Elizabeth asked incredulously.

"Actually, there never was a woman or a message," Arielle lied. "The pendant was a birthday present from Uncle Yvan, but I just didn't want to say he was the one who had given it to me."

Elizabeth shook her head furiously as if denying what she was hearing, and then glared at Arielle.

"What's going on? Why won't you just tell me the truth?" Liz said sharply.

The bus turned off the main road onto Fieldview

Street. The next stop was Emmanuel's. Arielle felt her heart begin to race. The bus stopped in front of the post office. The door opened to admit a half-dozen students, including Emmanuel, as well as a blast of cold air. The long-haired teenager took the seat behind the two girls. A flush crept into Arielle's cheeks, and her mouth went dry.

"Good morning, ladies!" Emmanuel greeted them brightly.

"Hi there," replied Elizabeth. Arielle found herself unable to speak—or even move. Her tongue was frozen in her mouth, and her limbs had gone limp. Luckily she had been sitting down; otherwise, she would have crumpled to the ground as her knees turned to jelly.

"Arielle, are you OK?" Emmanuel asked.

"Uh…yes," she replied monosyllabically.

Elizabeth studied her companions closely, her eyes flicking from one to the other. She suspected—and rightly so—that something was going on between those two.

ARIELLE'S English teacher, Mr. Gordon, was a short, colourless and nervous man. Not a hair grew on his pear-shaped head. His round and slightly bulging eyes, like those of a fish, constantly darted from side to side behind the lenses of his glasses, which seemed thick enough to stop a bullet. He hurried across the classroom and dumped the papers he was carrying into a pile on his desk. He then went to the blackboard and wrote:

ALTER EGO

"Can someone tell me what this means?" he said, turning around.

No-one put their hand up.

"Anyone?"

Silence.

"This is a Latin term that means 'another self'," explained the teacher. "What is the connection between this term and the book you are reading?"

Rose sat on Arielle's right, and Elizabeth on her left. Turning to her friends, Rose shrugged and mouthed, "I did not read the book." Arielle giggled.

Mr. Gordon called upon Elizabeth, who had raised her hand.

"My Hyde is Dr. Jekyll's alter ego," Elizabeth said proudly.

"Correct," said Mr. Gordon. "As you continue reading, you will see that the theme of the book is duality. Two very different personalities share the same body. One is clearly good, but what about the other?"

"The other personality is evil," Elizabeth chimed in.

"Excellent! Ms. Quintal is right. Mr. Hyde is thoroughly evil and is everything that Dr. Jekyll is not. I would like you to focus on this concept as you finish the book. Pay close attention to the differences between Jekyll and Hyde. What distinguishes one from the other? Why are the personalities opposite of one another?"

Arielle thought about Elleira and the Alters. There was a strong similarity between the novel she was reading for her English class and her recent adventures. Could Hyde have been Jekyll's Alter?

"Mr. Gordon, what would happen if we really could separate good from evil?" asked the boy sitting behind Arielle. The teacher smiled.

"Good question. Does anyone have any idea of what *could* happen?"

Judging by the class's response, apparently not a soul.

Mr. Gordon put his piece of chalk down, adding, "I

believe you will find the answer by the time you finish the book."

AT the end of class, the students got up and left the room. Elizabeth had to go to the washroom, so she told Arielle and Rose she would catch up with them later. The two girls nodded and headed to their lockers.

"So what's up with that girl who looks like you?" asked Rose eagerly.

"Actually, she was only part of a nightmare I had that seemed very real," replied Arielle, hoping to sound as convincing as possible.

"A nightmare?!"

"I sleepwalk sometimes. I must have filmed myself with my uncle's video camera that last time," Arielle went on, mentally crossing her fingers. But Rose was no fool.

"Is that the best excuse you can come up with? Listen, Elle, if you don't want to talk about it, that's fine. Just don't take me for an idiot."

At that moment, Arielle spotted Emmanuel at the end of the hall; he was coming towards them. He raised his hand in greeting and smiled at Arielle as he walked past. Rose waited until he was out of earshot before turning to her friend.

"Is that the guy who almost got into a fight with Simon and Noah at lunch yesterday?"

"Yes."

"Do you know each other?"

Arielle did not know how to respond.

"Well, do you?" Rose insisted.

"Oh, not really," Arielle finally replied.

Rose did not believe her.

"Whatever. He has a nice smile, though," added Rose.

"You think so?" said Arielle.

Rose laughed.

"There's no mistaking that smile he gave you. And look at you: your cheeks are bright red."

Again, Arielle was speechless. Rose was right. Arielle had felt her temperature shoot up when Emmanuel had approached them.

"I think Liz has a crush on him," confided Arielle.

"So? That doesn't mean he's her property."

"Rose!"

"What? I like Liz, but she doesn't have a chance with a guy like that," protested Rose.

"That's not really fair to her," Arielle said in Elizabeth's defense.

"Did you see him? He looks like Johnny Depp from *Pirates of the Caribbean.* What makes you think he would be interested in *our* Elizabeth, the plainest girl in school? That's one match-up that won't be happening anytime soon."

"I couldn't do that to her."

"Well, does he like her?" asked Rose.

"I don't think so," said Arielle.

"Do you like him, then?"

"I'm not sure…"

"That smile he gave you is a pretty clear sign of how he feels about you," Rose noted.

"Yeah, maybe."

The girls finally reached their lockers. They dropped off their English books and grabbed what they needed for their next class.

As they walked down the hall, Arielle turned to her friend.

"Rose, I have something to tell you, but you have to promise not to tell Liz."

"I promise," said Rose.

Arielle looked around to make sure Elizabeth was nowhere nearby.

"I'm going to Emmanuel's house to do my homework," she whispered.

"His house?" Rose said in astonishment.

Arielle nodded.

"You go, girl!" Rose squealed.

CHAPTER 11

History was the last class of the day.

Arielle, Elizabeth and Rose had heard through the school grapevine that they would be having a sub—news of a teacher's absence always spreads like wildfire through the student body. To the class's delight, the substitute teacher granted everyone a free period. The three friends decided to go to the library. When they arrived, they saw that another group of students was present. Simon Vanesse and Noah Davidoff were among them.

The girls sat at a table with six seats at the back of the room. Rose took out her copy of *Dr. Jekyll and Mr. Hyde*—she had some catching up to do. Elizabeth began doing the optional exercises assigned by Hellgebra (as she was affectionately known), the sadistic math teacher whose real name was Ms. Helen. Arielle also took out her math book and started solving equations. After a few minutes, she raised her head and spotted Simon and Noah, who had moved to the table across from hers. They were both staring at her silently. Arielle looked down at her book, unable to hold their gaze. Her friends also noticed the two boys' behaviour.

"Simon keeps staring at you," whispered Elizabeth.

Arielle raised her head again. Simon and Noah were still sitting there looking at her, but they did not say anything. Neither had moved a muscle. After a moment, they glanced at one another, closed their books and stood up.

I hope they won't ask to sit here, Arielle thought frantically.

"It looks like they're coming this way," Rose announced quietly.

"Hello, ladies," said Simon softly so as not to disturb the other students in the library.

"Hello," answered Rose and Elizabeth in unison.

Their voices carried a little too much, which earned them a stern gaze and raised eyebrow from the library monitor in the middle of the room.

"How are you, Arielle?" asked Simon.

Rose and Elizabeth turned to their friend, a look of surprise on their faces. By some miracle, Simon Vanesse, the captain of the hockey team, was actually *speaking* to one of them.

"How are you?" he repeated his question.

Arielle stared at him. She was positive that it had been Simon and Noah's Alters who had set the Dobermans on her the night before.

Rose gave Arielle a look that said, *What are you waiting for? Say something!*

"I'm fine," Arielle spoke in a monotone.

Simon smiled at her, but Noah remained impassive.

"I would like to talk to you," he said. "Just you and me."

Simon wanted to talk to Arielle *alone*?! Liz and Rose couldn't believe their ears.

"Would you like us to give the two of you some

privacy?" asked Rose helpfully.

"We could go sit at another table, or even in another room," offered Elizabeth.

For quite some time, Arielle had been telling her friends that she was in love with Simon Vanesse, so she couldn't blame them for their gushing enthusiasm. Apparently, the other two girls believed Simon's sudden interest in Arielle was their friend's big chance. Arielle would have certainly felt the same way—twenty-four hours ago.

"I was thinking we could go over there," said Simon, indicating the rows of bookshelves in the alcove at the back of the library, where student couples went to steal a kiss during school hours.

"No-one would see us. How about it?"

Arielle did not trust him.

"What do you want, Simon?" she asked suspiciously.

Her two friends were stunned. Arielle could guess what they were thinking: *She's crazy, she'll ruin everything!*

"I just want to talk," he insisted.

"Just talk, huh. Is that all?"

"It's OK, Arielle, I understand. Are you afraid of me?"

"You tell me, Simon. Should I be afraid of you?"

Simon glanced at Noah, and then focused his attention on Arielle.

"I really like you," he said.

"Oh, yeah? Since when?" she retorted.

Rose couldn't contain herself any longer.

"Stop it, Arielle! What are you doing?"

"Let her be, Rose," said Elizabeth, "this is none of our business."

"I wasn't talking to you, Liz," snapped Rose.

Rose and Elizabeth kept arguing in heated whispers.

"Are you coming with me or not?" Simon asked impatiently. He clearly had had enough of the other girls' spat. Arielle realized that the only way to calm things down was to accept Simon's offer.

"OK, let's go," she said.

Noah made to join Simon and Arielle, much to her annoyance.

"Why does *he* have to come along if you just want to talk to me alone?" she asked.

Simon told Noah to go back to their table and then led Arielle across the study hall to the reference section in the alcove. Simon ducked between the first two rows of shelves, but Arielle stopped. What would happen if she went with him? Noah knew she had the pendant, which meant Simon probably knew as well; after all, the two boys were best friends. Emmanuel had said that the Alters would try to recover the pendant. Had Simon been ordered to take it because Alters cannot manifest themselves during the day? That would mean Simon was in contact with his Alter, like Elleira had been with Arielle. How much of a hold did Nomis have over his Dayform, anyway? Did Simon do whatever his Alter told him to without question? Had he received instructions in a video like she had a day earlier?

"Don't you trust me?" asked Simon, standing between the rows of books.

"No," she replied.

"Do you think I've got something to hide?"

"What do you mean, Simon?"

He gestured with a curled finger that he wanted her to come towards him.

"I want to tell you something up close and personal," he said throatily.

It was obvious what he was hinting at. Arielle blushed. Although she was suspicious of his motives, she could not deny that he was very good looking.

She had lost track of the number of times she

wished he would take her in his arms in front of the whole school and kiss her passionately. She couldn't even remember when Simon *wasn't* the last thing she thought about before going to sleep, or the first thing she thought about when she woke up in the morning. And now he was standing only a few feet away, beckoning to her, but she could not bring herself to go near him. Why was she holding back?

Because her heart belonged to someone else: Emmanuel.

"I can't, Simon."

"Are you scared?"

She studied him for a moment.

"I'm just Arielle Queen, a fat little redhead who your girlfriend Lea likes to call Pumpkin. I don't have anything to offer a guy like you."

"Actually, I think you have a lot to offer," he said.

Simon strode up to her and grabbed her hand. Arielle allowed herself to be dragged between the bookshelves.

"See? This isn't so bad, is it?" the boy said soothingly.

Simon leaned forward to kiss her, but Arielle turned her head away at the last moment. She had a gut feeling that she should not let herself be seduced by Simon's smooth talking. He pulled her close, pressing his body against hers. He began stroking her cheek before slipping one hand behind the nape of her neck. With his other hand, he began groping under her shirt. Arielle felt uncomfortable.

"What are you doing?" Her voice was a shrill whisper of fear and indignation.

Simon lifted his head and stared at her. She did not like the look in his eyes.

"Where's the pendant?" he hissed.

He seemed angry. In a flash, Arielle understood why he had brought her to this isolated part of the library.

"You just want the pendant, right?" she asked disgustedly.

Arielle was furious with herself for being so naïve.

"Where is it?" he repeated.

"I'm not wearing it today."

"Is it at your place?"

Arielle tried to back away, but he seized her and yanked her towards him.

"Where is it, Arielle?" Simon began tightening his grip.

The teenaged girl felt her terror mounting.

"Let go, Simon! You're hurting me!"

He ignored her plea.

Arielle glanced over her shoulder to see if anyone had noticed she was in trouble—and spotted Emmanuel at the end of the row.

"Let her go or else," commanded Emmanuel.

Simon burst out laughing.

"You think I'm scared of you, you little dork?" Simon shot back.

"You ought to be," retorted Emmanuel, his hands curling into fists as he strode towards the struggling pair. Arielle felt both relieved—and flattered. Her very own knight in shining armour had come to her rescue!

"Get your hands off her," growled Emmanuel. "Or you're gonna get hurt."

As the long-haired teenager continued his threatening advance, Arielle had the impression that he was actually *glowing*. Oddly, this did not frighten her; in fact, it made her feel safe.

"You're not tough enough to take us both on, freak," said a voice behind Emmanuel. Arielle craned her head and saw Noah Davidoff standing at the end of the row, at the very spot Emmanuel had vacated just seconds earlier.

"Your guard dog is well trained," said Emmanuel

through clenched teeth.

Noah was blocking the only exit leading back to the main room. Did he expect Emmanuel to back down? What would happen if Emmanuel made good on his threat to attack Simon? Would Noah tear into her rescuer as savagely as his Dobermans had tried to the night before?

"They're both Alters," announced Emmanuel after studying the other boys' faces.

Neither Noah nor Simon responded.

"How did you manage to do that, guys?" Emmanuel asked. "Only the most powerful Alters can take control of their human forms during the day."

At that moment, Mr. Burr, the library monitor, loomed up behind Noah. His permanent scowl and no-nonsense manner were a result of a long stint in the army.

"What's with all the chatter?" he barked in a tone reserved for snot-nosed recruits. "*Silence* isn't just a seven-letter word; it's one of the rules. Now break it up!" With that, he turned smartly on his heel and marched back to his post in the middle of the study hall.

"You're both lucky that Sarge was there," growled Simon. He released his grip on Arielle and shoved her towards Emmanuel, who caught her in his arms.

"Are you all right?" he asked.

She nodded.

"Noah, let them leave," ordered Simon. "We'll settle this later."

Noah stepped aside without a word. With a sweeping gesture, he indicated they were free to go. Emmanuel and Noah glowered at one another.

"You almost got me last time," said Emmanuel crisply as he walked past the other boy. "Oh, yeah—thanks for the draugur sword. I always wanted one of those."

True to form, Noah did not react.

Arielle and Emmanuel kept glancing over their shoulder at the other boys as they wove through the tables in the main reading area on their way to the exit.

"Thank you," said Arielle once they were outside the library.

Emmanuel put his arm around her shoulders, drew her to him and kissed her on the cheek.

"That was close," he whispered in her ear.

Startled—and thrilled—by this display of affection, Arielle simply blushed.

"I was keeping my eye on them all day," explained Emmanuel, releasing her. "I had a feeling they were up to something. It's a good thing you weren't wearing the pendant."

"Yeah. I left it at home in the secret closet with my Alter outfits," she replied, struggling to keep her emotions in check. She was sure her face was a deep red, but Emmanuel didn't seem to notice.

"Smart move. Are you still up for coming over to my place tonight to do your homework?" he looked at her expectantly.

"Sure!"

"Great! We won't take the school bus. My grandmother will pick us up."

Arielle was relieved. Now she wouldn't have to worry about making Elizabeth suspicious if she got off the bus at Emmanuel's stop.

"It wasn't really Simon and Noah back there, was it?" Arielle asked.

Emmanuel shook his head. "No, it was Nomis and Razan."

Arielle was puzzled. "I thought Alters only took control of their human hosts at night."

"Usually that's the case, but some Alters manage to dominate their host during the day. That's called 'integral possession.' Luckily, it doesn't happen often."

Emmanuel fiddled with his owl bracelets before continuing.

"Integral possession is permanent. Once the human personality has been pushed aside, it can never regain control of its body. It usually fades away after a few hours."

"Fades away?" Arielle gasped. "Then that means…"

Emmanuel nodded grimly.

"That means that the human personalities of Simon Vanesse and Noah Davidoff are probably both dead."

Chapter 12

A Chevrolet stopped in front of Arielle and Emmanuel.

To say the car wasn't a recent make would be an understatement—it was practically an antique...

Emmanuel's 80-something-year-old grandmother, whom he usually called Saddington, was driving the car. She was a shrivelled yet wiry creature with grey, dusty skin and a look of authority deeply etched into her lined face. Her tarnished spectacles teetered on the bridge of her hooked nose. She had her age-yellowed hair in a bun and didn't wear dentures. Her overall appearance was that of some small animal that had been trapped and skinned and mounted long ago and now sat, forgotten, at the back of a storeroom in a museum someplace.

The two teenagers climbed into the car, Arielle in the back seat and Emmanuel in the front. "Hurry up and close the door," croaked the old woman. "It's freezing."

Saddington eyed her passenger in the rear-view mirror.

"Arielle Queen. It's a pleasure to meet you."

Saddington gripped the steering wheel like an eagle

seizing its prey. The thick, ochre fingernails at the tips of her bony fingers seemed as sharp as claws. Arielle had the impression that the old woman would suddenly turn around and scratch her face.

"I've slashed more than one Alter in my time with these, young lady," said Saddington hoarsely, aware that Arielle was staring at her hands.

Arielle smiled weakly, not knowing how else to respond.

"Let's go," said Emmanuel.

Saddington turned her attention away from her passenger, and the Chevrolet began moving. In less than ten minutes, the trio were pulling into the driveway of Saddington's house. Arielle recognized the neighbourhood. She lived only a few streets away.

"What a pretty house," said Arielle as the car came to a halt.

Emmanuel got out first and walked around to the driver's side. He opened the door and offered his grandmother an arm to lean on. Thanking him, she grabbed his arm for support and pulled herself up.

"Pass me my cane, dear," Saddington said to Arielle.

Spotting the walking aid lying between the two front seats, Arielle grabbed it and handed it to the old woman. Firmly gripping the cane handle, Saddington released Emmanuel's arm and slowly made her way to the front door, accompanied by her attentive grandson.

Arielle got out of the car and stretched. After seeing his grandmother to the house, Emmanuel returned to the car and gallantly offered to carry Arielle's bag.

"Saddington is going to make us some hot chocolate," Emmanuel told her.

"Great! I like hot chocolate," replied Arielle.

They smiled at one another and began to walk to the house. Arielle studied Emmanuel out of the corner of her eye. The leather bracelets he wore caught her attention.

"Those are nice," she said, pointing to the boy's wrists.

"Thanks. Saddington gave them to me."

"Those are owls on them, right?"

Emmanuel nodded.

"Owls hunt by night, and so do I," he announced proudly.

They took a few more steps in silence.

"Do you have a lot of homework to do?" asked Emmanuel.

"No, not really."

"Sick! Then we'll have more time to talk."

"Talk about what?" Arielle was puzzled.

"About you. I want to get to know you better."

"Me? Why?"

"Why not? I didn't think you'd mind."

Arielle stopped.

"No. It's just that, well, boys aren't usually interested in learning more about me."

"Really?" said Emmanuel, startled. "I find that hard to believe."

"I don't," Arielle replied glumly, glancing down at herself. "I know what I'm worth—at least when I look like this."

"You're too hard on yourself. I think you're really pretty," he said reassuringly.

Arielle couldn't believe her ears! Did he just say she was pretty? She blushed as deeply red as she had outside the library that afternoon. Never in her whole life had she ever felt so happy, tingly and excited.

But then those feelings vanished as quickly as they had appeared. A guy as cute as Emmanuel couldn't possibly find *her* attractive. Short, wide and dumpy was never "the type" for tall, dark and handsome…

"Can we talk about something else?" she said self-consciously.

"Did I make you uncomfortable?" he asked.

"A little," she confessed.

Emmanuel smiled sympathetically. When they reached the house, he held the door open and motioned for her to go inside.

The house was a snug, yet older building, its age evident in the low ceilings, narrow hallways and small rooms. The tasteful décor and furniture gave the place a homey feel. Arielle had the impression of being in a dollhouse.

"Here we are," said Emmanuel when they entered the dining room. Craning his head towards the doorway, he called out, "Do you need a hand, Grandma?"

"No, thank you," came the reply from deeper inside the house. Saddington was surely in the kitchen preparing the hot cocoa. Emmanuel removed his math textbook from his backpack and set it on the table. Arielle did likewise. They sat across from each other and began working on the exercises assigned by Hellgebra.

Saddington hobbled into the dining room a few minutes later, clutching the handle of her cane with one hand and carrying a steaming pot in the other. Emmanuel reached out behind him to grab two mugs from the hutch. The old woman poured the hot cocoa into the mugs and sat down.

"There, now," she said. "Hurry and drink it up before it gets cold."

Arielle took a sip; it was delicious.

"This is the best hot cocoa I've ever had," she gushed.

"Thank you, dear," rasped Saddington. "So, young lady, Emmanuel tells me that you have a half-moon pendant. Is that true?"

Arielle glanced at Emmanuel, as if to draw strength from his gaze before answering.

"Yes, it's true," said Arielle.

"The pendant isn't a fake?" asked the old woman.

"It's the real thing," said Emmanuel. He then explained to his grandmother that Nomis, the Alter of Simon Vanesse, had threatened Arielle that afternoon in the school library. Nomis had obviously been after the pendant.

"A daytime attack? Do you think it was integral possession?" Saddington asked.

Emmanuel nodded.

"Is anyone else possessed?"

"Maybe Noah Davidoff," replied Emmanuel.

Saddington mulled over this information.

"Two cases of integral possession in the same town," the old woman spoke without looking at either teen, like she had forgotten she was not alone in the room. "It seems this little nest of Alters may be a lot more than it appears."

"One pendant is here in Glory," added Emmanuel. "Do you think the second is here as well?"

Saddington scratched her pointy chin as she stared off into space.

"Possibly," she said. "I would even say probably."

The old woman remained deep in thought another moment before addressing the two young people.

"Do you realize what this means? The prophecy is starting to come true."

Saddington turned to Arielle.

"Firth Hinna Atta: the Journey of the Eight. This prophecy is written in the first chapter of the Book of Amon, the Dark Elves' holy text. According to the prophecy, the two Valinn and their six protectors will overcome all of the Alters and Sylphors. They will then travel to the Land of the Dead to fight the forces of evil and conquer Helheim. Their victory will only be complete when the two Valinn become one."

It was clear by the look on Arielle's face that she did not know what to make of the old woman's tale. Saddington seemed surprised at the girl's reaction.

"You do know that Alters and Dark Elves are creatures of the night, don't you?" asked Saddington gently.

Arielle shook her head.

"I didn't have time to tell her everything to her, but I said you would," said Emmanuel.

Saddington sighed. "Very well. Let's start at the beginning…"

THE old woman explained that the tall and agile Dark Elves have nothing to do with the dwarves and trolls they are often associated with in Norse mythology. According to legend, Dark Elves were sent to Midgard, which is our Earth, by Loki and Hel, the two evil gods who freed them from their prison in the Land of the Light Elves, Alfaheim.

For many years, the Dark Elves were the soldiers of Loki and Hel on Midgard, clashing again and again with the humans created by Odin. But the Dark Elves eventually rebelled against their masters and threatened to invade the Land of the Dead, where Loki and Hel live in a mighty fortress. Having lost control of their forces, the two gods had no choice but to go to Asgard and beg Odin for help.

Worried that the Dark Elves would invade the other eight worlds, Odin lent Loki and Hel the souls of some of his best human warriors to track down and eliminate the Dark Elves on Midgard. Loki and Hel created an army of Alters by exploiting the dark side in humans, using evil to fight evil. For an Alter to exist, the soul of its human host must be split into two personalities, both very different from one another, but sharing the same body.

"DOES everyone have an Alter?" asked Arielle once Saddington had finished.

"No," Saddington replied, shaking her head. "Alter hunters refer to people who are the host of an Alter as the 'Hugar Numinn', which means 'mind that is taken' in Old Norse. Every Hugar Numinn is a human possessed by the soul of a warrior Odin sent to help Loki and Hel. The ability to host an Alter has been passed down for centuries from grandfather to grandson and from grandmother to granddaughter. This ability always skips a generation."

"So my grandmother was probably a Hugar Numinn, too?"

"Yes," said Saddington, "and she must have hosted an Alter who also fought the Dark Elves."

"Have the Alters won many battles against the Elves?" asked Arielle.

"For now, the Dark Elves have the upper hand and hold most major cities. The last few battles were terrible, bloody affairs; the Alters were nearly wiped out. The Alters have all fled to the countryside, but the Dark Elves will soon hunt them down."

"And you tracked the Alters all the way here?"

"Yes."

"Why do you hunt Alters and not Dark Elves? The Dark Elves seem to pose a greater threat."

"There are already many first-rate Elf hunters. Our speciality," Saddington indicated herself and her grandson, "is hunting Alters."

"What if the Alters decide to rebel, like the Dark Elves did?"

"Odin demanded that Loki and Hel prevent that

from happening. He wanted to be sure that the Alters could be neutralized quickly if they got out of hand. That is why Loki created the half-moon pendants. If the two pendants are ever brought together, every Alter would immediately disappear from the face of the Earth."

Saddington licked her lips before going on.

"After making the pendants, Loki gave them to a group of his worshippers he knew would not hesitate to bring the two pendants together at his command. Their descendants passed the pendants down from generation to generation, until they were attacked by demon hunters in 1150 A.D. One of the hunters stole the pendants, but he was never found—even Odin does not know what happened to the man. Legend has it that he established the Mjolnir Brotherhood, which later became the Order of the Elding Knights, a secret society made up of the world's best demon hunters."

"Do you think the pendants will ever be joined?" Arielle asked.

"Yes, according to prophecy," said the old woman. "In a sacred text called the Book of Amon, it is written that 'The Alters shall disappear from Midgard, the Land of Men, after vanquishing the renegade Elves, for only then shall the two half-moon pendants form a perfect circle. The Eight shall commence their Journey after liberating Midgard from its enemies and travel to Helheim, the Land of the Dead. There, the Eight shall fight the legions of darkness, and emerge triumphant.'"

"This means the Alters will win the battle against the Dark Elves," Saddington explained, "but they will be destroyed when the two Valinn bring their pendants together. Once the Alters and Dark Elves are gone, the Earth will finally be rid of evil. The two Valinn and their six protectors will then fight Loki and Hel to free the souls trapped in their dark kingdom."

"Who are the six protectors?"

"According to the ancient texts, they are powerful warriors."

"Do you think I am one of the two Valinn?"

"Perhaps," said Saddington. "There is one way to be sure. Do you have a birthmark shaped like a butterfly on your right shoulder?"

How did she know that? thought Arielle with surprise.

"Yes, I do."

"May I see it?"

Arielle rolled up her sleeve, exposing her birthmark. The old woman examined it.

"Alters always have a butterfly-shaped birthmark on their shoulder, but it is usually brown."

"Mine is white," remarked Arielle.

"The prophecy says that the two Valinn will bear a mark purer than that of other Alters," Saddington added. "I think this is clear proof of who you really are."

Arielle's pale birthmark meant she was one of the two Valinn from the prophecy. She didn't know if she should be thrilled—or worried sick!

"Who is the second Valinn?" the girl asked.

"The one with the other half-moon pendant, my dear," replied Saddington. "But no-one knows who it is. We have to find out, and soon, because all of the Alters and Sylphors will literally move heaven and Earth to get their hands on the two pendants. Their survival depends on it. The Dark Elves need the pendants to destroy their enemies, and the Alters want the pendants to prevent the Sylphors from exterminating them."

"Razan and Nomis know I have one of the pendants," said Arielle.

"Is it in a safe place?"

"I think so."

Saddington turned to her grandson.

"It's hidden in her house in a secret closet," said Emmanuel.

"That should do for now," she said. "But we will have to get it soon. It must not fall into the hands of any demon, either Sylphor or Alter. Both sides must continue to slaughter one another, as it says in the prophecy."

"You didn't say anything about Animalters," Arielle pointed out, "can they be trusted?"

"Animalters simply exist to serve their Alter masters, and as far as I know, they are unable to betray them. Did Elleira have an Animalter?" asked Saddington.

"A cat."

"In theory, it should remain loyal to you. Note that I said *in theory*. If you ever begin to doubt about which side the cat is on, do not hesitate to get rid of it. Wait until it is in its animal form—it will be easier to dispose of it then," Saddington sighed. "I think I will go lie down now. I am tired."

The old woman rose. Before heading to the kitchen, she stopped and looked at Arielle.

"Don't you worry, dear. We'll take good care of you."

Arielle smiled at her. Emmanuel waited until his grandmother had left the room before sliding over to the seat next to Arielle.

"Everything will work out, you'll see," he reassured her.

"Really?"

He nodded, "That's what the prophecy says."

He then winked at her, and the two of them continued their homework.

Chapter 13

Emmanuel parked Saddington's car in front of Arielle's house.

The sky had turned pink as the sun began to set. It would be dark soon. Arielle's uncle used to tell her, "Beware of things that go bump in the night." After that night's events, however, those "things" would forever have a name: Sylphors and Alters…

Emmanuel turned the ignition off and looked at Arielle.

"Are you OK?" he asked.

"Yes," she said. "Do you think the Dark Elves know I have one of the half-moon pendants?"

"My grandmother doesn't think so. And she knows what she's talking about. You can trust her."

"What will Nomis and Razan do now?"

"They won't try anything tonight, as that would raise the Sylphors' suspicions. If the Alters suddenly began showing a lot of interest in you, the Elves will realize that you have the pendant—and that is one thing the Alters want to avoid at all costs. You should be on your guard as of tomorrow morning. Once the Dark Elves return to their hideouts, Nomis and Razan will do anything to get their hands on the pendant."

"The Dark Elves only come out at night?"

"Both the Dark Elves and Sylphors draw their strength from the moon," explained Emmanuel. "They are powerless in sunlight."

"What should I do if I am attacked by Alters?" she asked nervously.

"Basically, you have two choices: run away or fight. You can kill an Alter or Dark Elf by cutting off his head or stabbing him in the heart with a draugur sword."

"I hope I never have to do either of those things," she shuddered.

Emmanuel looked Arielle straight in the eye, and smiled. Slowly, their faces began to be drawn together, as if by a magnet. Their lips were now almost touching. Arielle felt her pulse pound in her temples and an intense heat burn deep inside her. She thought that if she did not kiss Emmanuel soon, the heat would spread through her body and consume her.

Arielle leaned towards Emmanuel, pressing her lips to his, gently at first, and then more firmly. She had never experienced anything so tender and yet so intense.

After a few seconds, they pulled away from one another. The closeness they had shared but a few heartbeats earlier had been replaced by a deep chill.

"We kissed…" mumbled Emmanuel.

Arielle stared straight ahead, afraid of what Emmanuel would think. She did not want him to have the impression she was "easy," which couldn't be further from the truth. In fact, this was her first kiss.

"Yes, we did," said Arielle tensely.

The teenaged girl did not dare move. She was certain Emmanuel would tell her to forget what just happened.

"Did you like it?" he asked.

She nodded hesitantly. "Yes."

"Do you want to do it again?"

"Seriously?"

He smiled and leaned towards her. He stroked her cheek and placed his mouth on hers. Their lips made contact once more. Their second kiss lasted several seconds.

"Your lips are soft," he murmured when they had stopped to catch their breath. "Just like your skin."

"Under all my freckles?"

Emmanuel laughed.

"I like all your freckles."

Arielle laughed, too. They kissed a few more times.

"I have to go," she said. "My uncle is probably wondering where I am."

It was a lie. Given the time, her uncle was most likely asleep on the living room sofa.

"Already?" asked Emmanuel, disappointed.

A little voice in the back of Arielle's mind told her she should get out of the car now to preserve the memory of her first kiss. She had to slip away before something or someone ruined the moment.

"See you tomorrow, then?" he added.

Arielle was thrilled by his question, which meant that he did not regret what happened. She was sure he would be dreaming about her all night, just like she would about him. Life can be unpredictable sometimes. Just yesterday, she couldn't stop thinking about Simon Vanesse, but now she wished she had never laid eyes on him. Why? Because Emmanuel Bolinger—who she had not even liked when they first met—had come into her life.

"Yes, I'll see you tomorrow," she said.

They kissed one last time.

When Arielle got out of the car, she had the impression she was ten pounds lighter. She hurried towards the house, certain that if she had been in her Alter form, she would have floated away.

ARIELLE was right: Uncle Yvan was already asleep, this time in one of the armchairs rather than in his usual place on the sofa. An empty bottle of vodka lay by his feet.

The young girl tiptoed over to the staircase and went upstairs. The house was getting darker by the minute, but she didn't dare to turn on a light until she had gotten to her room. When she reached her destination, she slipped inside and fumbled for the light switch. The bulb in the ceiling light fixture fizzled for a moment before blinking to life. Arielle noticed a huge lump under her bedspread as she put her bag down.

"Arielle, is that you?" the lump asked in a muffled voice.

"Brutus, what are you doing there?" Arielle replied.

The lump squirmed before answering.

"I was caught off-guard when the sun set," came the sheepish response.

Glancing out the window, Arielle noticed that the night had indeed fallen.

"I don't control my Altermorphoses as well as other Animalters do," explained the lump. "But it isn't just me—my six brothers have the same problem."

Arielle started to lift a corner of the bedspread.

"Don't! I'm not wearing anything!"

With a burst of laughter, Arielle let the bedspread drop.

"It isn't funny!" The lump protested.

"Sorry," she apologized between giggles.

"Instead of standing there making fun of me, why don't you get my clothes out of the secret closet?"

"Sure," Arielle replied, wiping the tears from her cheeks. "A streaker isn't much of a bodyguard anyway."

"Pffftttt," went the lump, getting in the last word.

Still chuckling to herself, Arielle lightly pressed the yellow butterfly on the flowered wallpaper. The hidden panel slid open. The teenager's eyes were immediately drawn to the pendant, which was still in the little niche by the silver cylinders where she had left it that morning. Carefully, she lifted the pendant out and slipped it around her neck—she felt like admiring her slim Alter body before going to bed. What type of girl did Emmanuel prefer: fat redheads or shapely brunettes? The answer seemed obvious.

"Don't you have my clothes yet?" asked the lump impatiently.

Arielle grabbed Brutus's outfit from the closet, brought it back to the bed and placed it in the furry hand sticking out from under the sheets. The hand withdrew, clutching its prize. Arielle put on her Alter outfit by the closet while Brutus got dressed under the covers.

"Where were you last night, Brutus?"

"Don't ask!" came the grumbled reply. "I nearly didn't make it back."

He threw the covers aside and stood up. As he put on his belt and adjusted his clothes, he filled Arielle in on what had happened at Bombyx Manor after they were separated. The Alters had originally fought back against the Sylphors. When it was clear they were outnumbered, Nomis sounded the retreat. Then it was every man for himself.

"I hid in the kitchen and waited for things to quiet down," he added. "The Elves left the manor not long afterwards. I think they chased the Alters all the way into the woods."

Arielle remembered there had been a man who had called to her as Elleira was taking control of her body. She clearly remembered the tone of his voice and his exact words. Obviously, he had wanted to help her, but had he managed to do so?

"Were you the one who helped me escape?" she asked.

"No, we got separated in the crowd."

"Who helped me, then?"

The Animalter shrugged.

"Did you know that Elleira had a boyfriend?" she said, changing her line of attack.

"Yes."

"We went to the manor yesterday because she wanted to meet him. Maybe he was the one who helped me."

Brutus fidgeted, but said nothing. Clearly, this subject made him uncomfortable.

"I can't tell you, Mistress," he answered, weighing each word carefully. "Not yet, anyway."

Arielle couldn't believe Brutus was not willing to share such important information.

"Oh, really? And why not?"

"I promised I wouldn't tell," he said.

"You promised *who* you wouldn't tell? Razan? Nomis? Elleira's boyfriend?"

Brutus did not respond.

"I need to know whose side you're on, Brutus!" Arielle raged. "The Alters—or mine? Look, I'm wearing the half-moon pendant. According to the prophecy, I'm one of the two Valinn. The Alters won't stop until they get it. I'll need your help to make sure they don't!"

"I will protect you and the pendant, Mistress. There is no need to worry about that," he assured her. "But I need you to trust me about why I can't say any more for now."

His whiskers twitched nervously.

"You should take your Alter form. We have to leave."
Arielle sighed, frustrated by all of these secrets.
"Where are we going?" she said curtly.
"There is someone I'd like you to meet."
"Could this *someone* answer my questions?"
"I hope so, Mistress."

Chapter 14

Standing in front of the mirror, Arielle spoke the words inscribed on the pendant, "Fra Retla! Fra Alter!" and watched her transformation…

Arielle's hair darkened as it grew longer, her face became thinner and her features more defined, her limbs stretched out and her muscles grew firmer. The rest of her body flowed and moulded to properly fill out the Alter outfit she wore. Within seconds, Elleira's stunning and graceful form was staring back at her in the mirror. This time, however, the process was painless.

"Perfect!" said Brutus. "We can go now."

"Who is this person who wants to speak to me?" Arielle asked the were-cat.

"A friend. He wants us to meet him at the football field by the school."

"How will we get there?"

Brutus flapped his arms. "How else?"

The telephone began to ring. Arielle answered.

"Hello?"

"Arielle, is that you? I'm at the front door with Eli. Can you let us in? I knocked earlier, but I guess no-one heard."

It was Rose calling from her cell phone. Arielle put her hand over the receiver and whispered to Brutus.

"My friends are at the front door. What do I do now?"

"Tell them to go home!" Brutus whispered back.

Arielle quickly came up with an excuse to get rid of Rose.

"Uh, Rose, my uncle is asleep. He might wake up if I have friends over."

"Arielle, open up!" ordered Rose. "Liz knows about Emmanuel. She saw the two of you together. I have to talk to you because she seems really upset."

Arielle placed her hand over the receiver again and whispered to Brutus, "It's Rose. She wants to talk to me *right now.*"

"Gimme that!" snapped Brutus, grabbing the receiver out of Arielle's hands. "I'm sorry, but Arielle is busy at the moment," he spoke into the phone in his most pleasant voice, "please call again later!" And he promptly hung up.

Arielle stared at Brutus incredulously for several seconds.

"I can't believe you just did that!" she exclaimed. "That was an important call! Rose said Liz was very upset because she had seen Emmanuel and me together."

"I didn't have a choice. We're already late!"

"Rose won't give up that easily. She'll wake my uncle up and make him open the front door."

"That doesn't matter," said Brutus. "We'll be long gone by then."

Brutus pulled on his coat before striding over to the window. He fumbled with the lock and tugged the window open with a couple of jerks.

"Let's go," Brutus said, glancing over his shoulder at

Arielle. He turned back to the window—and froze. There was Elliot, who had climbed up onto the garage roof to get to Arielle's room, no doubt at Rose's insistence. The Animalter and the teenaged boy stared at each other for a second—and then, pandemonium. Elliot leaped back with a yell, lost his footing and tumbled to the ground. Luckily, the cedar hedge below broke his fall.

"There's a giant cat in Arielle's room!" he shouted from the shrubbery.

Meanwhile, Brutus had retreated to the wall opposite the window, his hand clutching his chest over his heart and his eyes wide with shock.

"I think I just lost my first life," he gulped.

"Arielle, are you all right?" Rose called up. "Arielle, answer me!"

Arielle drew closer to the window, but made sure she stayed partially hidden behind the curtains so that Rose could not get a good look at her from the yard. It was a good thing, too, since Rose would not have recognized her friend in her Alter form.

"I'm OK," Arielle replied. "Don't worry."

"Run, Arielle!" yelled Elliot, who was still trembling like a leaf. "There's a mutant cat in your room!"

"Arielle, is there anyone up there with you?" Rose asked impatiently.

"No," Arielle laughed, "just Brutus."

"But this cat was at least six feet tall! And he was wearing clothes!" Elliot insisted.

Arielle smiled as she imagined the look on Rose's face.

"OK, fine," Rose snapped. "Tony the Tiger is hiding in Arielle's room! Happy? Can we be serious now, please?"

Flustered, Elliot fell silent. *Smart move, Eli*, thought Arielle. Making Rose angry was never a good idea.

"Elle, can you come down here? We have to talk

about Liz."

Arielle turned to Brutus and waited for his opinion.

"OK, go see her, but change back to your Dayform first," he advised.

Arielle opened her mouth to say the spell of transformation when she heard a scream from outside. She craned her head to look out the window.

"Rose?" Arielle called down.

"Who are those people?!" Rose shrieked.

"Rose, what's going on?" Arielle shouted.

"Get back," Elliot ordered an unseen party. "Stay away from us!"

With typical feline grace, the Animalter bounded to the secret closet and ducked inside. He appeared a second later holding a number of silver cylinders.

"Take these," he said to Arielle, tossing two of them to her. She easily snatched them out of mid-air with her heightened Alter reflexes.

"These are acidus injectors," he explained. "The tip contains a small quantity of acid that can dissolve metal."

"What for?" she asked.

"To pierce the armour the Dark Elves wear under their clothes to protect their torso," Brutus replied, leaping out the window.

Arielle's stomach knotted in fear. Were there really Dark Elves outside?

Quickly, the young girl climbed out the window onto the garage roof and lay beside Brutus. To her amazement, her eyes adapted almost immediately to the darkness. Her developing powers now included night vision, just like that of a cat or owl.

Glancing over the edge of the roof, she spotted Elliot and Rose to the right. Rose was hiding behind her boyfriend, who was holding his arms out protectively. The two of them were slowing backing away from the street, where three men and three women were watching the scene. They looked like Dark Elves. Arielle guessed they were after the half-moon pendant.

Arielle tightened her grip on one of the acidus injectors.

Bring 'em on! she thought courageously. *I'm ready for 'em!*

Chapter 15

Brutus pointed at one of the Dark Elves with an acidus injector.

"You have to aim at their chests, over the heart," he whispered to Arielle. "As soon as the tip touches the armour, the acid will melt a hole in it, and then the contents of the cylinder will be injected directly into the heart."

"What's in the cylinder?" she whispered back.

"Light Elf tears, which are poisonous to Dark Elves. Stab a Sylphor with one of these babies, and he just shrivels up and dies."

Shrivels up? thought Arielle, wrinkling her nose in disgust. *Ew, gross!*

The teenaged girl trembled, despite herself. She glanced to the right. Rose and Elliot had stopped and were staring in her direction.

"Who's up there?" Rose called out, trying to sound brave.

There was no need to hide in the shadows any longer.

Arielle jumped into the air. A gust of wind suddenly blew up from beneath her, easing her gently to the ground. Brutus followed suit, taking a defensive position to Arielle's left upon landing.

"It's me," she said.

"What happened to you?" gasped Rose.

"It's a long story."

Elliot looked her over from head to foot.

"Wow, have you been working out or what?" he grinned approvingly.

"I could use a hand over here, Mistress," yelled Brutus, stepping towards their foes.

"Told you," said Elliot over his shoulder as he pointed at the Animalter. "I bet that cat is juiced up on steroids!"

Arielle turned her attention to the Dark Elves. One of them slowly walked towards Brutus. The Elf was a tall, broad-shouldered specimen in his mid-twenties. He was rather handsome, with chiselled features. Arielle studied the six Elves and noticed they shared certain distinguishing characteristics: they all had pointy ears, black eyes and not a single hair on their heads. The baggy, ill-fitting clothing they wore made them look like a group of young thugs.

"Dark Elves gave up the Robin-Hood-men-in-tights look some time ago," snarked Brutus. "Now they dress like anarchists. Sure, their fashion sense may be more twenty-first century—but it doesn't make them any less dangerous."

Arielle noticed that the Dark Elf had a piece of paper in his hand.

"Two-three-zero Sphinx Street," he read aloud from the paper. "Is this the right house?"

That was Arielle's address! Someone had told him where she lived! It couldn't have been Nomis or Razan— Elves and Alters were mortal enemies. Then who?

"How did you get that address?" growled Brutus.

The Dark Elf ignored the question. He simply crumpled the piece of paper and tossed it on the ground.

"Stop!" ordered Brutus, waving an acidus injector in the Sylphor's direction. "Don't come any closer."

The Elf smiled stiffly and drew a long knife from under his coat. The blade glowed eerily.

"Look out! He's got a draugur dagger!" yelled Brutus.

"Why don't you just give me the pendant? It'll save us all a lot of trouble," said the Dark Elf to Arielle.

"Don't listen to him!" warned Brutus.

"Do you know who I am, girl?" he continued. "I'm Falko, the Voivod of the New World Clans. I am the most powerful Sylphor on the continent. This," he waved an outstretched arm in a sweeping motion, "is my kingdom. And that pendant belongs to me."

He burst out laughing as he sized up his opposition.

"To become Voivod, I had to eliminate many powerful rivals, so if you think one zit-faced teenager and her talking cat are going to stop me..."

Arielle was furious! *I may not be perfect, but I've never had bad skin!*

"Elle, what's going on?" said Rose.

Arielle could see the terror in her friends' eyes.

"Get out of here!" she yelled to them, pointing to the path between the garage and cedar hedge that led to the back yard. "It's not safe!"

"No-one is going anywhere unless I say so!" thundered Falko. He gestured to one of the other Elves, who leaped high into the air and landed just behind Rose and Elliot. The Elf pushed the boy onto the ground before grabbing Rose by the arms and pulling her towards him. Rose gave Arielle a pleading look.

"Let her go!" shouted Arielle. "She hasn't done anything!"

"Give me the pendant, and Hermod will release your friend," Falko said, his voice dripping honey.

Arielle glanced from Falko to Hermod. There was no way she would surrender the pendant, but she couldn't let anything happen to Rose. She raised her acidus injector. Brutus immediately understood what Arielle had in mind.

"Don't..." he protested.

But it was too late. Firmly gripping the silver cylinder, Arielle bounded at Hermod.

"Kill the hostage," ordered Falko.

Moving to obey, Hermod drew a dagger and brought it to Rose's neck. Luckily, Arielle managed to deflect the blow with her superhuman Alter reflexes and followed through with a punch to Hermod's face. The Dark Elf stumbled back, his arms flailing. *This is my chance!* thought Arielle. She plunged the acidus injector into Hermod's chest. It struck something hard, no doubt the armour Brutus had told her about. The acid in the tip instantly dissolved a small hole the size of a quarter in Hermod's shirt and in the armour he wore under his clothing. A small needle in the injector jabbed into his heart. Hermod gaped at Arielle as the Light Elf tears coursed through him, and then shrieked as his body crumbled and fell apart. Horrified, Arielle could not tear her eyes away as Hermod was reduced to a pile of dried limbs at her feet.

Elliot took advantage of this distraction. He ran over to Rose and helped her up.

"Run!" yelled Arielle.

Grabbing Rose's hand, Elliot dragged her down the path Arielle had pointed to earlier.

Arielle was sure Falko would not let her escape that easily. Brutus positioned himself between the Sylphor and Arielle—for all the good that did. Falko parried a few of the Animalter's thrusts before grabbing him and flinging him onto the neighbour's driveway. Arielle removed her second acidus injector from her coat pocket. She wielded it threateningly as Falko ran towards her, his draugur blade bathing his face in a bluish light. Their eyes met for a second. Arielle tried to turn her head from his crazed stare, but could not. Falko grinned maliciously.

The Dark Elf was going to chop her to pieces, and she knew there was nothing she could do to stop him.

Chapter 16

She watched helplessly as he charged towards her…

Every one of her heightened Alter instincts screamed at her to *move*, but she could not. Falko had managed to bewitch her. His foul spell had left her arms and legs paralyzed, and she found she could not look away from his penetrating gaze. The injector in her hand would not save her.

The blade of the draugur dagger was just inches from piercing her chest when she heard the beating of powerful wings. A huge raven suddenly flew between her and Falko. The dark-feathered bird gripped the draugur dagger with its claws and tore it from Falko's grasp. With a triumphant caw, it rose into the air, firmly gripping its prize. "The Alters!" yelled one of the Elves at their leader. "They're here!"

A short distance away, Arielle saw that a group of Alters—some holding acidus injectors, others armed with draugur swords—had formed a ring around the Sylphors. She recognized the Alters of Lea Darling and the CeeCees, as well as those of Oliver Guinness and William Louis-Seize, the loyal wingmen of Simon Vanesse. Razan, the Alter of Noah Davidoff, was leading the attack, his two Doberman Animalters at his side.

Falko had no intention of giving up, especially when so near to his goal. He reached out to grab Arielle's pendant.

"Get away from her!" thundered a familiar voice.

His coat flapping in the wind, Nomis hovered menacingly overhead. Suddenly, he plunged out of the sky and tackled Falko. The two rolled around on the ground, striking furiously at one another, until Falko grabbed Nomis by the waist and flung him violently away. Nomis easily righted himself in mid-air. Landing near the Dark Elf, he prepared to launch himself at his foe. Falko, however, had no intention of continuing the fight. With a mighty leap, he soared away.

"Coward!" bellowed Nomis. But Falko had already flown out of sight.

Arielle heard the wings of the large raven—most certainly an Animalter—as it circled once more before setting down near Nomis. The bird took on human form and gave the draugur dagger to its master.

"Follow Falko back to his rat hole," Nomis told the man-raven.

With a nod, the Animalter sprung into the air as it changed into a bird. It gave a loud cry, and then flew to the west as Falko had done.

The other Alters made short work of the remaining Dark Elves. Outnumbered, the Sylphors fell quickly, one to an acidus injector, the other three to the sharp blades of draugur swords. To kill an Elf, decapitation was as effective as an injector straight to the heart. Where but a moment ago stood four Sylphors, there remained nothing but small piles of withered limbs.

Arielle knew she was next. The Alters were going to finish her off now that the Dark Elves had been killed or driven away. But she would not escape without Brutus. Out of the corner of her eye, she spotted Brutus being pinned to the ground in the neighbour's yard by the two Doberman Animalters. As she moved to his aid, someone grabbed her from behind, an arm wrapped around her neck in a choke hold. She struggled vainly to break free. Judging by the size and strength of her opponent, she guessed her attacker was a man. He reached one hand around and fumbled roughly for the pendant she wore. Once he found it, he gave a sharp tug, snapping the chain.

"I have it," he said in a neutral tone.

Nomis smiled in satisfaction.

"Perfect," he said. "You can let her go now."

Finally free, Arielle turned to face her assailant. There was no mistaking the scar on his cheek: it was Noah Davidoff. Or rather, Razan. They stared at each other. His eyes did not betray any emotion, but she hoped he could see all the hatred she felt burning in her soul as she glared at him. Without the pendant, she could not stay in her Alter form. Already, she felt her body begin to change. Razan watched as she transformed back into Arielle Queen—the small, fat, little redhead with a face full of freckles. She shrank several inches, and Razan, keeping his eyes locked on her, had to lower his head to follow her Altermorphosis.

Arielle tried to back away from him, but she stumbled, tripped up in her clothing, which was now too loose in some places and too tight in others. She lay face first on the ground, humiliated and helpless.

"Why do fat girls always wear such tight clothes?" The snide comment came from Ael, Lea Darling's Alter.

The other Alters burst out laughing.

"You gotta be hot if you wanna wear leather pants," snarked Revilo. "She looks like a lumpy piece of carrot sushi!"

More gales of laughter. Arielle couldn't take it anymore and burst into tears, which, to her tormentors, added to the hilarity of the scene.

"Give me your hand."

Arielle raised her head. Razan had extended his hand towards her. There was no way she would let him help her up if it meant exposing herself to further ridicule.

"Go on, take my hand," he repeated his offer.

Unlike the other Alters, he did not laugh. His features remained as impassive as ever.

"Hurry and help her up so we can get this over with!" growled Nomis impatiently.

Razan seized her arm and pulled her to her feet. His strength was impressive.

"Let's put the pendant in the safe," said Nomis. "It's the only place where no-one else can get their hands on it."

"I'll take care of it," said Razan. "You and the others go after Falko. You're all better trackers than I am."

Nomis mulled over his lieutenant's suggestion.

"All right," he said. "Ael and Revilo will stay with you."

"There's no need for that. I've got Geri and Freki."

"Suit yourself," said Nomis with a shrug. "We'll meet up later at the manor. Don't forget to get rid of that girl and her Animalter." Pointing to the remains of the Elves, he added, "And clean up that mess."

"No problem," said Razan.

Arielle's throat clenched. Had she heard correctly: were they really planning on killing both her and Brutus? *What were you thinking?* she silently berated herself. *These are demons—they're pure evil. They just turned four powerful Elves into piles of dust. Do you think for a second that they're going to have any qualms about killing some fat girl and her cat?*

Nomis, Ael and the other Alters flew away one after the other, leaving Brutus and Arielle at the mercy of Razan and his two DoberMen.

Razan waited until the last of the Alters had disappeared before turning to Arielle.

"Don't worry, Venus," he told her. "Me and the dogs aren't going to hurt you."

He undid the first few buttons of his shirt to reveal something hanging around his neck.

It was the second half-moon pendant.

CHAPTER 17

Arielle could not mask her look of surprise.

"Are you OK?" Razan asked.

Arielle was too shaken to respond. She had been certain that she was going to die at his hands, but now he was giving her reason to believe she would live to see the next sunrise.

"Don't worry, Venus. You're safe now."

The DoberMen released Brutus, who immediately rejoined Arielle.

"Gracias," said Brutus to Razan. "I was starting to think they would never leave."

So Brutus and Razan *had* been up to something. Arielle turned to her Animalter. It was clear from her scowl that she wanted an explanation.

"Not here," said Brutus. "Let's go up to your room."

Before Arielle could respond, Brutus had scooped her up in his arms and leaped to the garage roof. Razan and the two DoberMen joined them a moment later. They all entered Arielle's bedroom through the open window. Arielle had begun to get chilly in the fall night air; it struck her that she had lost her Alter form's resistance to the cold when the pendant was taken from her. She pulled her bathrobe on for warmth.

"This is the friend we were going to meet," Brutus announced.

Razan nodded, adding, "I was about to leave to go meet you when one of the Alters' informants warned us that Falko and several other Elves were planning on attacking you tonight. Nomis was worried the Sylphors were after the pendant, so he rounded up a group of Alters to stop them."

Arielle sized up the young man.

"You're wearing the other half-moon pendant," she said. "Does that mean you are not Razan?"

"Yeah, I'm really Noah," he replied. "Razan is tucked away somewhere inside me, but I can control him with the pendant."

"Does Nomis know you have it?"

He shook his head.

"The only ones who do are in this room. The other Alters think I'm still Razan."

"So you're just putting on an act, then?"

"Yeah, but I won't be able to keep it up forever. Nomis isn't stupid—he'll notice something's different about me sooner or later."

"And I suppose you are the other Valinn?"

"I guess so."

"Show me your birthmark."

Noah took off his coat and unbuttoned his shirt to reveal a telltale butterfly.

"The birthmark is brown," remarked Arielle.

Noah licked the tip of his thumb and rubbed his birthmark. A gooey, brown substance, like fine mud, appeared on his shoulder. He wiped it away with the palm of his hand to reveal a white butterfly.

"I use my mother's makeup to darken the birthmark,"

he explained. "If the other Alters knew my butterfly birthmark was white, they would realize I am one of the two Valinn."

Arielle was quite upset. "But what about me?" she said. "They already *know* I am the other Valinn! Are they going to keep chasing me clear across the country?"

"They won't be able to find you if you hide," Noah reassured her.

"Hide? Hide *where?*"

"I rented a room at the Apollo Motel. You can spend the night there. I'll come and get you tomorrow night."

"And then what?" Arielle was shouting, more scared than angry. "Hide somewhere else the night after that? How long do I have to keep running?" She punctuated her speech with finger thrusts at Noah. "I have a life to live: school, my friends. I don't want to become a fugitive at sixteen!"

"Nomis has to believe that I killed you and Brutus like he ordered me to," replied Noah evenly. "If we want him to think you're both dead, you'll have to drop out of sight."

Arielle's insides were clenched with anxiety. She trembled when she realized her daily routine, once so predictable and safe, was no longer either of those things.

"But what if we joined the two pendants together right now?" she suggested. "We could eliminate all of the Alters in one swoop, and the Dark Elves would probably leave us alone."

"And leave the Earth in the clutches of the Dark Elves?" Noah retorted. "Not a chance. The prophecy clearly says that the two pendants will be used to destroy all of the Alters, but only after they have wiped out all of the Sylphors."

"Noah, I can't hide forever! There must be thousands and thousands of Dark Elves all over the world. It would take years to destroy them all!"

"We'll figure something out, I promise. The balance of power between the two groups of demons is shifting. The fact that a Voivod like Falko is in Glory is a sign the Sylphors are planning something big. I bet they're going to attack soon."

"Look at this," said one of the DoberMen handing Noah a piece of paper.

"Falko threw that on the ground earlier. My address is written on it," Arielle added.

Noah showed it to her. It read:

She lives at 230 Sphinx Street
E.Q.

"Do you know anyone whose initials are E.Q.?" asked Noah.

Arielle thought for a moment. There was Elise Quenneville, the older sister of Jolene Quenneville, but Elise was staying at a boarding school at least two hundred miles away. There was also Ernest Quigley, the mayor's brother. She doubted it was him, though. Ernest was the town drunk who, according to rumour, couldn't read or write.

"Elizabeth Quintal!" exclaimed Brutus.

"What?" Arielle gaped at her Animalter.

"E.Q. is Elizabeth Quintal!" repeated Brutus. "Rose said that Elizabeth was upset because she had seen you and Emmanuel together, right?"

"Upset enough to tell the Dark Elves where you live?" Noah suggested.

Arielle was furious. She *knew* Elizabeth, and her best friend would *never* betray her.

"Elizabeth doesn't know any Dark Elves. She isn't even aware they exist!" Arielle raged.

"Are you sure?" asked Noah.

"It's not her!" Arielle said emphatically.

Noah mulled this information over.

"You should pack a bag. We'll have to leave for the motel soon."

"My uncle will call the police tomorrow morning when he finds out that my bed was not slept in all night," Arielle pointed out.

"Then you'll have to write him a note saying you slept over at a friend's place," said Noah.

Arielle was not keen on spending the night at a motel, but she could not deny that it was far too dangerous for her to stay at home. Resignedly, she grabbed a bag from the closet and began stuffing clothes into it.

"So what do we do about Elizabeth?" Brutus directed the question to Noah.

"We'll deal with her," Noah said in his customary monotone.

Arielle's head snapped up.

"You keep your hands off her!" she thundered, jabbing a finger at the Alter.

"Don't tell me what to do, Venus," replied Noah.

"Leave my friends alone! I don't want them dragged into this mess! And don't call me Venus!" Arielle shouted.

"Someone told the Dark Elves that you have one of the half-moon pendants. My job is to find out who," Noah replied.

"It wasn't Elizabeth!"

"We'll see about that."

Noah zipped Arielle's bag up and slung it over his shoulder.

"Hey, I'm not done!" she protested.

"You have enough clothes to last a month. Hurry up and write that note for your uncle. We'll wait for you outside."

Noah climbed out the window, followed by the DoberMen. The three of them vanished into the night.

Arielle clenched her teeth and fumed.

"Who does that guy think he is anyway?"

Chapter 18

The Apollo Motel was on the other side of town.

They decided travelling by air was the best option. Noah and the DoberMen flew in the lead. Brutus followed, carrying Arielle on his back.

It took them barely ten minutes to reach their destination. As a precaution, they circled the premises from the air before gently landing in a poorly illuminated corner of the parking lot. Noah hurried to the motel office and returned a few minutes later with a key.

"You're in room 23," he announced, giving the key to Arielle.

"Where did you get the money to pay for the room?" she asked.

Noah took a thick wad of bills out of his pocket.

"My dad's loaded. He won't miss this," he said, wagging the money. "Here's an extra $300. I left a cell phone and a bag of snacks in the room in case you and your cat get hungry."

Arielle took the money and stuffed it in her pocket, certain that, sooner or later, it would come in handy.

"I have to speak to you privately," said Noah, gesturing at the door to her room.

She unlocked it, and they both entered. Noah closed the door behind them.

"Geri and Freki will take their animal form after I leave and keep watch outside the door. You'll be safe here," he assured her.

"Where are you going?" Arielle asked dryly.

"To try to find out who E.Q. is," he replied, placing her bag on the bed.

"What are you going to do with my pendant?"

"Leave it in the manor safe. Nomis checks it every day. If he doesn't see the pendant there tomorrow morning, he'll know something's up."

The two young people fell silent. The lull in the conversation stretched from uncomfortable to awkward.

Taking a deep breath, Arielle addressed the source of their unease.

"Are you the one who gave the pendant to Elleira?"

The boy nodded.

"I had the two of them for a very long time," he said.

"Where did you get them?"

"From this guy who is an Elding Knight."

Arielle looked at Noah sceptically.

"What's an Elding Knight?"

Noah explained that the Order of Elding Knights was a secret society founded by Ulf Thorvald, the demon hunter who had stolen the pendants centuries before. Thorvald had founded the society under the name Mjolnir Brotherhood. Their mission was to protect the pendants and fight Dark Elves and Alters. Noah added that the man who had given him the pendants was one of Thorvald's descendants.

"The knight told me that the second Valinn was a girl," continued Noah. "I wouldn't have to find her—one day, she would come to me. And when that day came, I had to give her the pendant. During a party at the manor one night, I saw that Elleira's butterfly birthmark was white like mine, so I knew you were the other Valinn. I gave the second pendant to Elleira, which would let you control her, just like I control Razan."

Noah stared into Arielle's eyes as he spoke.

"At first, Elleira didn't understand why I was giving her the pendant, but when she realized that you were the other Valinn, she threatened to tell Nomis. But she came up to me a little later and agreed to keep the pendant secret. She said that something made her change her mind at the last second. She thought that something was you, Arielle."

"Me?" said Arielle, startled.

"The Alters are a part of us. You influenced Elleira's decision. I believe you made her change her mind and help me."

"Why would have I done that?"

"Maybe because, deep down, you're in love with me."

"Say what?" Arielle stared at Noah incredulously. "*Me*? In love with *you*?"

She couldn't keep from smiling at the very idea that she, Arielle Queen, was in love with Noah Davidoff. She would have burst out laughing, but didn't want to hurt his feelings.

"You're wrong there, Noah. Elleira was the one who was in love with you, not me. And being in love with you is what got her killed. That won't happen to me, that's for sure."

"You might end up like her if you keep hanging around Emmanuel," said Noah.

He had gone too far this time! It took all of her self-control not to slap him.

"Leave Emmanuel out of this!" she roared.

"You shouldn't trust him. I think he is one of the Dark Elves' Kobold servants."

"A Kobold WHAT? There's more of them?" Arielle laughed bitterly. "Hey, what's one more creep in this little freak show?"

Noah ignored her outburst. "A Kobold is a human who's being changed into a Dark Elf. The Elves use Kobolds to guard their rat holes during the day and to spy for them at night. You can tell a Kobold from the dagger-shaped burn scar on their wrist; being branded with a red-hot iron is part of the process for becoming a Dark Elf. To protect themselves from Kobolds, powerful Alters developed the ability to take control of their human hosts through integral possession."

Noah fidgeted for a few seconds while studying Arielle's face. Taking a deep breath, he forged ahead.

"Last night at Bombyx Manor, I think Emmanuel was scouting out the grounds for the Sylphors. When he saw you run out of the manor, he must have noticed you were wearing the half-moon pendant, so he followed you. Do you understand what I am trying to tell you? Emmanuel wasn't trying to save you, Arielle—he was trying to get the pendant."

"Sorry, Noah, but I don't believe a word," Arielle replied curtly. "Emmanuel has never threatened me. In fact, he helped me escape from the Dobermans *you* set on me, remember?"

"He's manipulating you to gain your trust, Arielle. He figures that if you think of him as a friend, you will lead him to the second pendant sooner or later. But his Sylphor master mustn't be very patient, which is probably why the Elves attacked you tonight."

"You're just making that up," Arielle shot back. "Who says that you aren't the one trying to manipulate me?"

She opened her bag and began pulling out her

clothes. She couldn't stand being in that ill-fitting Alter getup any longer.

"Arielle, don't let Emmanuel sweet talk you," begged Noah. "Haven't you noticed that he's always wearing leather bracelets? He's using them to hide the burn marks on his wrists."

"That doesn't prove anything. Those leather bracelets were a present from his grandmother!" Arielle said angrily. "What do you have against Emmanuel, anyway? It sounds like you're jealous!"

As she turned to finish unpacking, she sneered, "Maybe you're the one who's in love with me."

Noah drew nearer.

"Yes, I am," said Noah, looking Arielle in the eyes. "But that isn't the reason I'm warning you to be careful around Emmanuel."

Arielle froze.

"You–you're in love with *me*?" Arielle froze. It was the first time a boy had ever told her he loved her.

"Do you find that so hard to believe?" he replied.

Arielle cast her eyes downwards, unable to hold Noah's penetrating gaze. He quickly walked towards her, caught her up in his arms and kissed her. She tried to push him away, but he held her too tightly. All at once, a series of images flashed in her mind. Everything was jumbled at first, but she eventually recognized the entrance of Bombyx Manor. She watched herself walk through the front door with Brutus, as she had the night before. Noah was there, too, leading them to the ballroom.

The images were passing by so quickly, it was like someone had set her memory to fast forward. The ballroom doors opened. The same Alters she had seen the night before were dancing to the same techno beat. There was Nomis, standing on the stage in the middle of the room and inviting Elleira to join him. Shortly afterwards, the assembled Alters began to gather around her, chanting her name and clapping. The sound of an explosion interrupted the festivities. The music stopped. An Alter began to scream that the Sylphors were attacking. The windows shattered. Elleira told Arielle to take off the pendant. Arielle began to feel like a spectator in her body while Elleira grew stronger. The Dark Elves poured into the ballroom and charged the Alters. Everything began to go dim. Arielle couldn't move her arms and legs. The last thing she remembered was hearing a man's voice yell, "Over here, quick!"

Arielle now recognized the voice as Noah's. Although Elleira had taken control of Arielle's body after the teenager had removed the pendant in the ballroom, Arielle now realized that Elleira must have been too weak to wholly dominate her. Arielle's awareness had actually been floating on the very edge of consciousness the entire evening, but the memory was so faint she could not recall it before now.

Seizing Elleira's hand, Noah had dragged her to the far end of the ballroom. They ducked, unseen, behind the bar, where there was a hidden door that opened onto a staircase leading down into the cellar. The two young people slipped through, taking care to close the door behind them. Once downstairs, Noah sheathed his sword.

"Are you all right?" asked Noah, examining Elleira for wounds.

"I'm getting weaker by the hour," panted Elleira. "I'll be dead by sunrise."

"Elleira—I'm sorry."

"I gave the pendant to Arielle. The rest is up to the two of you."

"I don't know how to thank you."

A loud boom from upstairs echoed through the cellar.

"There's a tunnel at the back of the cellar that exits near the woods behind the manor," said Noah. "Once you get outside, head for the forest—it's your best chance. I'll stay here to cover your escape. I'll catch up with you later, if I can."

"Noah, I've done everything you wanted me to and have never asked for anything in return. But now, there *is* something I want: a kiss."

Noah pressed his lips against hers, wrapping his arms around in her in a warm and tender embrace. Elleira smiled when they drew apart, tears coursing down her cheeks.

"You have to go now," Noah whispered.

Elleira looked at him one last time before disappearing down the tunnel.

THE memory ended abruptly. Arielle opened her eyes and realized she was no longer struggling against Noah's grip. In fact, *she* was kissing *him*. Guilt washed over her—she felt she had betrayed Emmanuel.

"Stop!" she shouted, turning her face away from Noah's. "What have you done to me? Did you cast some sort of Alter spell on me?"

"No. No, I didn't…"

"Liar! Go away! Leave me alone!"

"Arielle…"

"I said GO!!!" Arielle commanded, pointing to the door.

Noah nodded sadly and left the room. After changing into her pajamas, Arielle let Brutus in.

"Are you OK?" he asked.

"What do you think?" she snapped.

Brutus took off his leather coat and threw it on the bed.

"Noah said he would be back tomorrow night."

"Good for him!"

"He thinks it would be for the best if you don't leave the room until he gets back."

"Noah Davidoff isn't the boss of me! I can do what I want."

The harshness of her tone made Brutus smile sadly.

"He's only trying to help you, you know," the Animalter said soothingly.

Arielle snorted.

"I don't trust him one bit!"

"Really? Why not?"

"Emmanuel told me to be on my guard around Noah."

"And you trust Emmanuel?"

"He saved me!"

"So did Noah."

Arielle sighed deeply. Her mind was a battlefield of conflicting thoughts; she couldn't tell her friends from her enemies anymore.

"I don't want to talk about it now," she said, "I'm exhausted. Are the two Dobermans still there?"

"The last time I checked, they were," answered Brutus. Turning his head to the motel door, he called out, "Hey, Scooby Doo, where are you?"

Irritated growls could be heard through the door.

"I hate those mutts!" Brutus hissed.

Chapter 19

Arielle fell asleep as soon as her head hit the pillow.

But a series of nightmares involving bloody clashes between Alters and Sylphors prevented her from getting any rest. For once, she was relieved when Brutus's meowing woke her the next morning. She slowly turned her head to look at her cat. Brutus had resumed his animal form and was sitting on the pillow next to hers. He began to gently lick her nose with his rough little tongue.

"Stop that," she mumbled groggily while pushing him away. "Brutus, please don't lick my nose anymore, OK?"

Brutus stared at Arielle.

"Don't look at me like that. We both know you're more than just a cat."

The clock-radio on her nightstand read 8 a.m. Arielle threw back the covers and got out of bed. The sun was shining through the partially opened curtains. The growling outside the door indicated the Dobermans were still at their post. Arielle guessed that they had returned to their dog form.

Arielle turned on the TV and began flipping through

the channels.

Nothing good on, she thought, lips pursed, *it figures.*

Her stomach gurgled at exactly 8:12 a.m. Taking an apple from the bag of food left by Noah, she ate it while watching an infomercial about some new gadget. With absolutely nothing to do, and it being only 9:30 a.m., she decided to go back to bed. Her sleep was, mercifully, more sound than it had been the night before.

The teenager woke up a little after 2 p.m. While munching on a few cookies, she decided to take a shower, get dressed and go out. She wanted to see Emmanuel and ask him what he thought about this Alter business.

Brutus guessed what Arielle was planning when she put on her coat. Slipping between her legs, he planted himself in front of Arielle's shoes. When she made to grab for her footwear, he hissed menacingly at her; clearly, he did not want her to leave the room.

"You won't make me change my mind," said Arielle, scooping up the cat and tossing him onto the bed.

Brutus meowed plaintively.

"Crying me a river isn't going to work, either," she added.

Arielle called a cab with the cell phone Noah had left her. She opened the motel door—and came face-to-face with the two Dobermans. Growling, they rose and blocked her path.

"Let me pass!" she said, her heart pounding.

A rumbled warning from deep in the dogs' chest was their only response. Neither budged an inch.

"What are you going to do? Bite me? Noah wouldn't like that, now, would he?" Arielle said sweetly.

She took a step forward. They snarled more loudly.

"Get out of my way!" she said firmly, aware that she had to quickly master her fear if she wanted to leave the motel.

Arielle squared her shoulders and took another step forward. Barking and growling, the dogs circled around her, but made no move to attack. *You can do it!* she told herself. She reached behind her and closed the door. She then wove between the guard dogs. So far, everything was going well. She slowly began walking towards the motel office, but then changed her mind and decided to wait for the taxi next to the parking lot entrance.

The dogs followed her all the way to the main road and posted themselves on each side of her when she stopped. She reasoned that she could get rid of her "bodyguards" when the taxi arrived. She was hoping the driver would not allow the animals into his vehicle.

Five minutes later, Arielle saw a white car turn the corner, the words "Glory Taxi" and a telephone number written on the front door. She waved to get the driver's attention. The taxi stopped in front of her.

"Sorry, Miss, no pets," called the driver out the partially lowered window.

Arielle grinned.

"No problem there."

Before the Dobermans could react, Arielle opened the door and slipped inside the taxi. Smirking, she blew them a raspberry through the window. The dogs responded by barking furiously.

"Dogs don't like it when their owner leaves them behind," remarked the driver as they pulled away from the curb.

"They aren't mine. I have a cat, and he's the only pet I want."

THE TAXI stopped in front of Emmanuel's house. Arielle glanced at her watch. Classes had ended a few minutes ago, so Emmanuel should be home soon.

"Are you getting out here or do you want me to wait?" asked the driver impatiently.

Arielle reached into her coat pocket and pulled out the wad of cash Noah had given her the night before. Peeling off two twenties, she handed them to the driver saying, "Will this do?"

The man's face lit up.

"Yes, ma'am," he said in his most pleasant tone. "How about some music?"

He held up an Elvis Presley CD.

"No, thanks," she replied.

An old Chevrolet appeared at the end of the street a few moments later. The car, with two occupants inside, passed the taxi and turned into the driveway of Saddington's house. Emmanuel, who was at the wheel, got out first and cast a curious glance at the taxi. Arielle smiled. Her joy was short-lived, however, when Emmanuel's passenger came into view: it was Elizabeth.

CHAPTER 20

Arielle couldn't believe her eyes! Emmanuel and Elizabeth—together?

The frizzy-haired teen couldn't just sit there! She needed to know what was going on between Emmanuel and Elizabeth. Those two had some explaining to do!

Without a word to the driver, Arielle opened the door and got out of the cab. She stormed across the street towards her friends. Could Elizabeth really be the E.Q. who wrote the note? Arielle was angry enough to believe it now. Angry—and maybe jealous, as well…

"Arielle? What are you doing here?" Emmanuel called out as he walked towards her. Elizabeth, her arms crossed, remained beside the Chevrolet and fixed Arielle with an unfathomable look.

"I searched everywhere for you, Arielle," Emmanuel went on. "I was really worried about you…"

"I see you don't like to worry alone," snapped Arielle.

"What?"

Emmanuel gaped at Arielle, but she had already focused her attention elsewhere. The boy glanced over his shoulder and understood what she meant. The two girls stood and stared at one another, murder in their eyes.

"Elizabeth was helping me," Emmanuel added.

"Helping you?" Arielle eyed Emmanuel suspiciously.

"I didn't know where you were," he explained. "I asked Elizabeth to show me your usual hangouts. We looked for you all over town."

So, they had spent the entire day together. That bothered her much more than she thought it would.

"Don't you realize that Elizabeth is in love with you?"

Arielle blurted out the words—and immediately regretted it. *I've just betrayed my best friend by telling one of her secrets*, she berated herself. *Why did I do that? Revenge? Did I want to get back at her for spending time with Emmanuel?*

"In love with me?" Emmanuel repeated. He glanced at Elizabeth before turning back to Arielle. "Er, OK. But why are you so angry?"

I don't know, thought Arielle. She wasn't sure if she even *wanted* to know, either, so she sidestepped the question.

"Brutus and I were attacked by Dark Elves last night," she said.

"What?! You're not hurt, are you?"

"No, thanks to a group of Alters who showed up at the last minute."

Emmanuel reached out and cupped her face in his hands.

"Is that why you weren't at school today?" he asked

Arielle nodded.

"I'm sorry," he sighed. "I should have been there."

Elizabeth looked on in silence.

"Someone told the Sylphors that I have the pendant. That's why they showed up at my house."

"Are you sure?"

"We think Elizabeth is the one who told them."

"Who is 'we'?"

She debated telling him about Noah and decided there was no point in sharing that information—yet. She felt it would be better to be cautious. Who knows? Maybe Noah was right, and Emmanuel was up to something after all.

"Brutus found a note with my address on it. It was signed E.Q. That's how the Elves knew where I live."

"I take it you think Elizabeth is this E.Q.?"

Arielle didn't respond, but Emmanuel guessed the truth from the look on her face.

"Now I understand why you are so angry," he said sympathetically. He gave Elizabeth another quick look. "I guess you think she led me on a wild goose chase, huh?"

"Let's ask her and find out," Arielle said curtly.

Arielle stepped around Emmanuel and walked towards Elizabeth, pounding out her fury with every step. Emmanuel trailed behind.

"Why did you do it?" The anger in Arielle's eyes erupted as she approached the girl she long considered her best friend.

"Do what?" replied Elizabeth, perplexed.

"Tell them I had the pendant!"

"What are you talking about?"

"I want the truth, Liz! Why did you stab me in the back?"

"You're the one who stabbed *me* in the back!" retorted Elizabeth. "I told you I liked Emmanuel, but you went after him anyway. I thought I could trust you."

"Don't change the subject! I know you're the one who told the Dark Elves where I live!"

"*What* did you say?"

Elizabeth's confusion seemed genuine. Could Brutus

have been mistaken? If Elizabeth wasn't the mysterious E.Q., then who had written the note?

"Is something wrong?" Emmanuel asked as he drew near.

Arielle hesitated, disarmed by Elizabeth's reaction.

"I-I'm not sure," stammered Arielle. "I think I made a mistake."

Elizabeth's eyes flicked from one friend to the other; she had absolutely no idea what Arielle and Emmanuel were talking about.

"Can we go inside?" Arielle asked Emmanuel.

"Sure," he replied. "I'll go tell Saddington you're here."

He hurried to the house. Elizabeth waited until he was out of earshot before speaking.

"It was stupid of me to think he was interested in me," she admitted. "You're the one he wants."

"Don't say that, Liz."

"It's true! I was with him all day. He was obviously very worried about you. It made me jealous. I'm sorry."

Worried about me or about the pendant? Arielle thought cynically. She felt a stab of anger at Noah for making her suspicious of Emmanuel.

"No, I'm the one who should apologize," Arielle said. "I doubted you, and I shouldn't have."

Emmanuel appeared at the front door.

"Hey! Saddington has cookies and hot chocolate for us!"

"Coming!" Arielle called back.

Elizabeth turned to her friend as they walked up the driveway.

"Was I hearing things or did you ask me if I had given your address to some *elves*?"

CHAPTER 21

There were four people gathered around the dining room table: Emmanuel, Saddington, Elizabeth and Arielle.

Arielle spoke first, telling Elizabeth everything about the Alters, the half-moon pendants, the prophecy, the Valinn, Falko, the Dark Elves and the bloody war the two groups of demons have been waging for centuries. She gave a detailed account of the events at Bombyx Manor and at her house over the past two nights. Detailed, but incomplete—she said nothing about Noah Davidoff beyond what she suspected Emmanuel already knew.

"Elves are real? What about orcs? I've always liked orcs more than elves!" Elizabeth babbled excitedly.

"Orcs are real, too," said Emmanuel.

Elizabeth smiled dreamily.

"Sick!" she exclaimed.

"If you say so," said Arielle.

"Let me get this straight," Elizabeth laid her hands flat on the table as she spoke. "You and the other Valinn have to wait until the Alters have killed all of the Dark Elves before bringing your pendants together, right?"

Arielle nodded.

"And when the two half moons will once again form a circle, all of the Alters will be destroyed. Then the two of you will go down to the Land of the Dead to fight Loki and Hel to rescue all of the souls they have trapped there! That is so awesome!"

"Thanks for making it sound so easy," Arielle replied sarcastically.

"Do you know who the six protectors are?"

"No, not yet."

"I bet they're tall and handsome warriors!" Elizabeth let herself be swept along in another romantic fancy. "Do you think I could go with you? To see the Land of the Dead, I mean?"

Saddington cackled. "You really don't want to go there, my dear. Only the souls of the damned, like Alters and Dark Elves, can visit Helheim and return to tell about it."

"So it's possible to come back from the Land of the Dead?" Elizabeth was full of questions.

"Just like it is possible to return from the kingdom of the gods," replied the old woman.

"*In this world, the body is only an anchor for the soul,*" said a voice from inside Arielle. It was not Elleira, either. The voice went on, "*When the anchor is raised, the soul can spread its wings and fly to any world it wants.*"

Whose voice is that? Arielle grew worried about this latest intruder in her mind.

"We have to find out who E.Q. is," Emmanuel stated matter-of-factly, setting down his mug. "Or else Arielle won't be able to live a normal life."

"I know who it is," Elizabeth piped up. "Elliot."

"Elliot *Rivard?*" said Arielle doubtfully. "Rose's boyfriend?"

"No," said Elizabeth, shaking her head. "Don't

you remember what Rose told us several months ago, about Elliot's mother making him take his stepfather's last name when she got remarried—to George Quaid? Elliot's full name is actually Elliot Rivard-Quaid. Elliot Quaid? E.Q.?"

"Bravo, Elizabeth," Saddington crowed. "Maybe that explains why Elliot was at Arielle's house last night. And maybe your friend Rose is involved, too."

"I don't believe that!" exclaimed Arielle. "The Dark Elves nearly killed them last night!"

"It only *looked* like the Elves were going to kill them, dear," said Saddington. "Sylphors and Alters are very good at that sort of trickery."

Perhaps Emmanuel's grandmother was right, but it would take more than maybes and what-ifs to convince Arielle that Elliot was the one who had given the note to the Elves. She wanted irrefutable proof. She had already falsely accused Elizabeth; she didn't want to repeat the same mistake with Elliot and Rose. And there was one other thing: was Emmanuel really a Kobold working for the Sylphors?

Arielle turned to Emmanuel.

"Can I speak to you privately?"

"Sure," he replied.

He led her upstairs to his bedroom and closed the door. Arielle felt uneasy about being alone with him in that particular room.

"I know who the other Valinn is," she blurted out, "I spoke to him last night."

Arielle hesitated, unsure of whether she should continue.

"He thinks you're a Kobold."

"Me? A Kobold?" Emmanuel was stunned. "Do you believe him?"

Arielle simply shrugged.

"Who is the other Valinn, Arielle?"

"I can't tell you," she replied.

"Arielle, who is it?" he insisted.

"Emmanuel, what are you hiding under your leather bracelets?" she said, taking over the role of interrogator. She was afraid she may have gone too far, but she had to know the truth.

"Does that mean you believe this guy?"

"Prove him wrong, and I won't."

Emmanuel looked crushed. Staring at her for a few seconds, he yanked off his leather bracelets and showed her his wrists. Nothing. Not the slightest trace of the dagger-shaped burn mark of a Kobold servant. Arielle lowered her gaze, ashamed of having doubted Emmanuel—and relieved she had the proof that Noah was mistaken.

"Happy?" he asked dryly.

She nodded.

"Who is the second Valinn?" he repeated his earlier question as he slipped his bracelets back on.

Arielle decided she could confide in Emmanuel. After this little scene, she felt she owed him that much.

"It's Noah," she admitted.

"Noah Davidoff? Are you sure?"

"He showed me his pendant."

Emmanuel shook his head at Arielle's claim.

"That's not proof, Arielle. It may have been a fake. In the short time I've been an Alter hunter, I've seen at least ten phony half-moon pendants. The Alters mass produce them to trick the Dark Elves."

"I think he was telling me the truth," Arielle insisted.

"Noah and his dogs almost killed us two nights ago, and you think he was telling you the *truth*?! That's kind of naïve, don't you think?" said Emmanuel.

"Noah said that it was you who were chasing me the

other night because you wanted to get your hands on my pendant."

"And you believe him? Do you honestly think that I would hurt you?"

Arielle did not know what to say.

"You weren't speaking to Noah, you were speaking to *Razan*," Emmanuel raised his voice to the point he was nearly yelling.

The teenaged girl was aware that she had hurt Emmanuel, as much by her words as by the things she had left unsaid.

"I don't know why he wanted you to believe this garbage," Emmanuel barrelled on, "but I'm sure he's got a reason. We have to tell Saddington. She's the only one who can help us figure out what the Alters are up to."

He walked to the door.

"Emmanuel, please…" Arielle begged him.

"There's no time to waste," was his curt reply before he walked out of the room.

SADDINGTON served them all another cup of hot chocolate.

"The Alters are trying to manipulate things," she said after Emmanuel had told her about his conversation with Arielle upstairs. "At least, it seems like that is what they are doing. By pretending to be the second Valinn, Razan is hoping to force the real Valinn to reveal himself. And when he does, the Alters will capture him and take his pendant."

Saddington turned to Arielle.

"The only reason Nomis left you alone with Razan was for him to gain your trust. That is how Alters get what they want: they lie and twist things. Never forget that Alters are demons, young lady. They are very, very clever. Sometimes all they need is to touch their victim once to weave their spell over him—or her."

Arielle recalled the conversation she had with Noah just before they kissed and he had told her he loved her.

"But what if we're wrong?" said Arielle. "What if Noah really is the other Valinn? He knew a lot about what is going on: the prophecy, the Mjolnir Brotherhood, the Elding Knights and the demon hunter who escaped with the pendants."

"When will you be seeing Noah again?" asked Elizabeth.

Arielle was suddenly unsure if revealing that information was a good idea.

"Tonight," she said slowly.

Emmanuel's eyebrows shot up in surprise.

"Where are you going to meet him?" he asked.

"I don't know if I should…"

"Arielle, our collective safety depends on you telling us," he said.

Saddington placed one of her wrinkled hands on Arielle's. "The Alters already took your pendant, dear. If our suspicions are correct, and they succeed in capturing the second pendant, they will become invincible. Bringing the two pendants together is the only thing that can banish them all from our world forever. If we do not stop them, they will destroy the Dark Elves and enslave humanity."

Arielle mulled over the old woman's words and decided she could trust her.

"Noah reserved a room for me at the Apollo Motel," she announced. "Room number 23. That is where he will meet me."

"You should stay here tonight," advised Emmanuel. "I'll go instead."

"No. Brutus is still over there, and I won't abandon

him."

"You're no match for Razan," he pointed out.

"He doesn't seem that tough," she countered.

"He is a *demon*. For all we know, he may have cast a spell on you."

Arielle had to admit this was possible. *Sometimes all they need is to touch their victim once to weave their spell.* Noah *had* touched her, and more than that—he had kissed her. She decided to not share this information with the others.

"I have to go now," she said, eager to end the conversation.

"I can take you back to the motel," Emmanuel offered.

"That's nice of you, but why don't you just meet me there later instead? How about showing up a little after sundown? I would like to talk to Noah alone first."

"What if he attacks you?"

"Brutus will be there."

"It could be a trap," cautioned Saddington. "Noah may bring other Alters with him. You and Brutus won't be able to fight them all."

Arielle smiled, despite herself. Their concern was touching, but she felt she should have a face-to-face conversation with Noah, regardless of the danger. She secretly hoped that Emmanuel and Noah were both wrong in suspecting each other's motives. Wouldn't it be wonderful if, by talking to Noah, she discovered that both boys were on the same side?

"I'll be fine," she reassured them. "There is nothing to worry about."

Arielle looked at Emmanuel.

"See you tonight," she added.

"I'll be there," he said.

"Could you call me a taxi, please?" Arielle asked her hosts.

"Elle, do you think I could hitch a ride?" Elizabeth chimed in.

Once the call was placed, the two girls thanked Saddington for her hospitality and got up.

"SO YOU really think everything is going to be OK?" asked Elizabeth as the two girls stepped outside.

"I'd like to think so," said Arielle. "But I'm not so sure anymore…"

They waited for their cab in silence.

Chapter 22

After dropping Elizabeth off at home, Arielle had the driver take her back to the Apollo Motel.

During the trip, she used Noah's cellphone to leave a message for her uncle. "Hi. I'm fine, don't worry about me. Be back soon." She tried to call Rose on her cellphone. No answer. She tried calling Rose's house, but she only got the voicemail. She dialled Eli's cell. Again, no answer. When she called his house, she was told he was out.

"Do you know where he is?" she asked.

"Am I his secretary? I got no idea."

Click.

GERI and Freki were pacing outside the motel office, but stopped when the taxi drove up. Arielle did not like the way they were looking at her when she got out of the car, but she walked towards them anyway, taking care not to give them a reason to attack her. If Noah had lied about his intentions, as Emmanuel and his grandmother believed, that meant the two Dobermans were actually there to spy on her rather than protect her. Who knows what they would do if they felt she was threatening them? Noah had probably given them instructions on what to do if she tried anything "funny."

The two dogs waited until Arielle had reached them before following her to her room. They then posted themselves on either side of the door. Arielle entered the room and saw Brutus sleeping on the bed. He stretched, hopped onto the floor and rubbed himself against her leg in greeting. He then jumped back onto the bed and sat looking at her like he was ready to listen.

"Do you want me to tell you about my day?" she sighed, sinking into an armchair.

Brutus meowed.

"Can I take a little nap first?"

He turned away and lay down on a pillow.

Arielle felt drained. She dragged herself out of the chair and flopped onto the bed. As she lay there, she kept thinking about Simon Vanesse, Noah Davidoff and Emmanuel Bolinger. Two days ago, she was madly in love with Simon, but her feelings changed completely once she found out who he really was. Emmanuel came into her life just as she began to lose interest in Simon. Had she let herself be seduced by Emmanuel simply to get over Simon? No, her feelings for Emmanuel were more than just a crush. But was it love? She may have believed that it was—before Noah came along. *He* was the one who ruined everything. *He* was the one who made her doubt Emmanuel's intentions, who made her wonder whether Emmanuel was her friend or her enemy. She was furious with Noah for calling her relationship with Emmanuel into question—and for saying he was in love with her! Was Noah telling her the truth about how he felt about her, or was he trying to trick her, as Saddington believed? But if she was so angry with Noah, why was she so troubled by the fact Noah claimed to be in love with her? Why should she even care? That was her last conscious thought before drifting off to sleep...

ARIELLE was awakened about an hour later by the cellphone ringing. She figured it was probably Noah or Rose. Arielle had left the cellphone number on the other girl's voicemail.

"Hello?" Arielle answered groggily.

"Arielle? Is that you?"

Arielle was right; it was Rose. A panicked Rose, no less.

"Elliot has disappeared!" said Rose frantically. "I haven't seen him all day! No-one knows where he is. Do you think the Elves got him? Will they be coming for me next?"

"Rose, calm down. The Dark Elves can't go out in broad daylight," Arielle spoke in a soothing tone before mentally adding. *But their Kobold servants can!* She decided to keep that information to herself.

"But it's going to be dark soon! They'll be back for me—I know it!"

Arielle craned her neck to look out the window. Sure enough, the sun was dipping below the horizon. Once the town was asleep, the Alters and Elves would creep out of their dens and continue to clash as they had for the past few nights. The two dogs and Brutus would also be able to take their Alter forms. *But not me*, she thought glumly. She was the only one involved in this supernatural war who would not transform at sundown.

While listening to Rose, she studied her reflection in the mirror on the wall: it looked like she had put on twenty pounds overnight! In the dimming light, her freckles seemed to have taken on a darker hue that disgusted her. She longed to assume Elleira's graceful form, if only for a few minutes. *No!* she corrected herself. *For a lot longer than that!* She would love to remain in her Alter form forever! She wanted that body to be hers—to be eternally beautiful…

"Are you still there, Arielle?"

Rose's question snapped Arielle back to reality.

"Yes, I am," Arielle responded hurriedly, trying to put her jumbled thoughts in order. "Listen, don't worry about the Elves. They were after me last night, not you."

I wish I could say as much for Elliot, Arielle thought. If Elliot was in fact the E.Q. who gave the Elves the note, did that mean he was a Kobold servant working for the Sylphors? If so, he was probably with his masters at that very moment. How would Rose react if she learned her boyfriend was a wannabe Dark Elf? It might break her heart, but you never knew with Rose. She might find it romantic.

"I have to go," said Arielle. "I'll call you later. Tell me if you hear from Eli."

"OK, Arielle," said Rose.

The two girls hung up. Arielle noticed a lump under the sheets after she got out of bed. It must be Brutus hiding in his customary spot before undergoing his Altermorphosis. *I guess modesty is a characteristic of the animal kingdom, too,* Arielle chuckled to herself.

"Do you want me to hand you your clothes?" she asked the lump. She interpreted the muffled meow as a yes. Arielle lifted a corner of the covers and placed Brutus's outfit on the fitted sheet. The cat reached out for the clothes with a furry gray paw and meowed in gratitude.

A loud noise from the bathroom drew her attention. The bathroom door was shut, so she couldn't see what had made the noise. This puzzled her, as she was sure she had left that door open after taking her shower earlier.

Another noise from the bathroom.

Someone was in there! Arielle knew she had to leave the room at once. She began backing towards the front door.

"Brutus, let's go," she called to the cat in an urgent whisper.

She wondered if the Dobermans were still outside the front door. With their keen hearing, they should have been alerted by the noise. But why weren't they barking? Weren't they supposed to protect her? Unless—Noah was still loyal to the Alters. If that were the case, the dogs would be the last ones she could count on for help.

Arielle had almost reached the front door when, to her horror, the knob on the bathroom door began to turn. She froze, transfixed, as the door slowly yawned open, like a black maw preparing to devour her. Arielle's throat clenched in fear, and her heart pounded like a jackhammer.

A silhouette appeared in the doorway. It was a man, judging by the size. Now she would learn who had been making those noises earlier.

"Step out where I can see you," she challenged the figure.

Having lost the element of surprise, the man tugged the door fully open and swaggered into the room. He was taller than Arielle and was wearing a ski mask, leaving only his eyes and mouth exposed. He wore jeans and a red, woollen pullover that seemed awfully familiar. One of his hands was hidden behind his back.

"Who are you?" she asked in as forceful a tone as she could muster.

"Who am I?" the man said laughing. "Someone you've been causing a lot of trouble for."

The voice was familiar, but she was too scared to identify it.

"I didn't think you would wake up so soon," he continued. "A few more minutes, and you wouldn't have felt a thing."

He pulled his hand out from behind his back to reveal a draugur sword. The weapon began to glow eerily in the growing darkness. *The sun has almost set. I have to buy myself some time until Emmanuel gets here,* Arielle thought.

"I didn't want you to suffer," he said. "I wanted your death to be quick, but then that stupid cellphone started to ring."

His eyes narrowed accusingly, and he lowered the sword until it was pointing at the floor. The light it cast illuminated the white Nikes he was wearing. Arielle could make out the word *Rose* written on the shoes in a fancy script.

"Elliot!" gasped Arielle.

The masked intruder did not react.

"Elliot, we're friends!" she pleaded.

"Shut up!"

"How about we just sit down and talk, OK?"

"I said SHUT UP!" he bellowed and lunged at her.

Arielle barely had the time to shield her face with her hands before Elliot was upon her. He knocked her arms aside and grabbed her by the neck.

"Eli, don't!" she choked out the words.

He raised her effortlessly with one hand and brought her close to him.

"I hope you enjoyed the sunset, because it is the last one you'll ever see!" he sneered.

Elliot tightened his grip, preventing Arielle from speaking. He brought the tip of the draugur sword to within inches of her chest and taunted her silently with her impending doom. Suddenly, there was a knock at the door.

"Arielle?" called a voice through the door. "Arielle, are you there?"

The young girl glanced at the door and remembered,

to her horror, that she had locked it before taking her nap.

"Arielle," insisted the voice. "Answer me!"

Taking advantage of this distraction, Arielle kicked at Elliot repeatedly and succeeded in making him drop his weapon. With a sweeping motion, Elliot threw Arielle onto the bed. She bounced on the mattress and sucked in air, relieved at once again being able to breathe.

Her respite, however, lasted no longer than the time it took for Elliot to pin her wrists beneath his knees while straddling her chest. He raised his sword above his head, a crazed look in his eyes. Arielle was petrified with terror. She was staring Death in the face, but the face was that of a friend. Elliot was about to take her most prized possession—her very life—and there was nothing she could do to stop him.

"See you in hell!" hissed the predator to his prey.

Squeezing her eyes shut, Arielle braced herself for the fatal blow. But the blow never fell. After waiting for what seemed to be an eternity, she snuck a peek and saw that Brutus, now in his Animalter form, had grabbed her assailant's arm, thus preventing the sword from striking her.

BAM! BAM! BAM!

"I'm going to break down the door, Arielle!" yelled the voice.

Arielle remained trapped beneath Elliot, who was struggling with Brutus. The were-cat was trying to drag the masked teen off Arielle, but Elliot refused to be budged. The blade of the draugur sword waved about wildly. Brutus held firmly onto the boy's sword arm, aware that if Elliot managed to break the Animalter's grip, both Brutus and Arielle would be killed.

Arielle wanted desperately to help Brutus. The pressure on her wrists lessened as Elliot tussled with the were-cat. Wriggling her hands free, Arielle immediately clawed Elliot' face, sinking her nails deeply into the ski mask and dragging her fingers downwards as hard as she could. Elliot cried out in pain as she tore into his flesh. Brutus seized the opportunity to yank the sword out of the boy's grasp and send him tumbling onto the floor. As the teenaged boy got to his feet, Brutus shoved him into a corner of the room.

Arielle was now clutching the ski mask, blood dripping from her fingernails. She looked at Elliot to see how badly she had hurt him, but it was now too dark for her to clearly make out his features.

Brutus had the sword pointed at the boy's chest.

"Chill, dude," said the Animalter.

Turning to Arielle, he added, "Mistress, turn on the light."

Arielle stumbled for the light switch on the wall and flicked it on. Her eyes adapted to the brightness in a couple of seconds. When she was able to get a good look at her attacker, she realized that he was not Elliot at all...

Chapter 23

The shock at this unexpected revelation was quickly replaced by confusion, which then dissolved into sadness…

"No, no, no."

The pain of the bruising she suffered during the attack paled to the dagger of betrayal that had been plunged into her heart.

"No, no, no."

She kept telling herself that her eyes were playing tricks on her, that her attacker was not someone she knew—and loved…

"No, no, no."

But it was undeniable: the man who had broken into her motel room was none other than Emmanuel.

Smiling evilly, he kept his eyes locked on her, like he was savouring every moment of her distress.

"The mark of the Kobolds you were looking for wasn't hidden by my bracelets," he jeered. "It's on the nape of my neck. Why do you think I wear turtlenecks all the time?"

Arielle said nothing. This turn of events was so horrible, it had to be a nightmare! The Emmanuel in this room couldn't possibly be the boy she had come to know and care for. Was he possessed? Hot tears welled up in her eyes and poured down her cheeks.

The hinges on the front door finally gave way as Noah burst into the room, draugur sword in hand.

"Arielle, are you all right?" he asked her worriedly.

Wiping away the tears, Arielle nodded, too overcome to speak.

"Are you sure?" he glanced over his shoulder at the broken door. "Someone drugged the dogs and…"

Noah stopped talking when he spotted Emmanuel.

"You! You're the one who drugged Geri and Freki!"

Emmanuel didn't dare move with the sword blade pointing at his chest.

"Are you really a Kobold servant?" she said to Emmanuel, still struggling to accept the identity of her assailant.

"Not for much longer," he boasted. "Falko elevated me from common human trash! He made me his heir. Look, my ears are already beginning to change. I'll be a Dark Elf soon!"

"Not if I can help it!" snarled Noah, who began to move towards the other boy.

"No!" yelled Arielle.

Noah halted and stared at her.

"You can't kill him," she said.

"Why not?"

"I want to know what he's done to Elliot. Look, he's wearing his clothes and shoes!"

Emmanuel laughed.

"What if I said he lent them to me?"

Arielle turned to their prisoner.

"You'd be lying," she replied as calmly as she could. "Elliot wouldn't give up his Nikes to anybody. They're a present from Rose. How did you get them?"

She took a few steps forward. Emmanuel would have done likewise if not for Brutus's weapon.

"Let's just say I didn't give him a choice," Emmanuel sneered.

"Did you beat him up?" she asked.

"No. I killed him."

Though he had lost his sword, Emmanuel had managed to wound Arielle once more. However, she did not react to this news, not wanting him to see how much his words had hurt her. Instead, she channelled her emotions into maintaining a look of disgust.

"Are you E.Q.?" she said coolly.

"Yes."

"Then your name isn't Emmanuel Bolinger?"

Before he could answer, a voice from behind Arielle said, "If you take away the –er at the end of Bolinger and rearrange the other letters, you spell the word 'goblin.' It's a synonym for Kobold."

Whipping around, Arielle saw her uncle standing in the doorway of the room. Her jaw dropped. What was he doing there? How did he even know she was at the motel?

"E.Q. stands for Emmanuel Queen," her uncle went on. His eyes had never been as clear as they were now. Arielle could tell from the way he was standing that he hadn't had a single drink.

"Emmanuel is your brother."

"My brother?" she gasped. That couldn't possibly be true—could it?

"When you were a baby, you were separated from your family to protect you," Yvan said.

Arielle's knees grew weak.

"Separated from my family?" Her head was spinning. "Are you saying my parents did not die in a fire?"

Yvan shook his head.

"Are they still alive?" she asked hopefully.

"I'll explain later. We have to go before the Sylphors arrive. They know that Noah is here and that he's the second Valinn. They're coming to take his pendant."

"But how do they know I have the other pendant?" It was Noah's turn to be surprised.

"Emmanuel told them," replied Yvan.

"What? How did he know that?"

"I told him," Arielle confessed. "I thought I could trust him. I was wrong. I'm sorry."

Noah was speechless.

"She stabbed you in the back, man," jeered Emmanuel. "She told me because she's in love with me."

"In love with *you?*" snarled Noah. "Shut your pie hole!"

"Yeah, she is. You should have seen the way we made out in the car last night!"

A wave of humiliation crashed down upon Arielle, sweeping her dignity away in a mighty torrent. She hung her head and wished the ground would swallow her up.

"But she's your sister! How could you do something like that?" Noah yelled angrily.

"She's not my sister! She's the ENEMY!" Emmanuel roared, his eyes flashing.

Noah strode towards the other boy.

"No! You're the enemy!"

"What are you going to do? Kill me?" Emmanuel taunted Noah.

"If that's the only way I can protect my friends, you bet I will," Noah replied.

"Protect your friends?" Emmanuel laughed. "You can't even protect your dogs!"

Noah scowled.

"If I were you, I wouldn't wait too long to take them to the vet. I think they ate something…ehhh," said Emmanuel, making the so-so gesture with his hand as he spoke.

Before Arielle could react, Noah had pounced on the other boy and smashed him in the face with the pommel of his sword. Emmanuel crumpled to the floor.

"That's just great," muttered Brutus. "Now who's going to lug that pointy-eared loser around? Lemme guess: the only conscious Animalter at the motel. No way, José!"

"Leave him here," said Yvan. "By the looks of him, he will soon be a Dark Elf. It would be too risky to bring him with us."

Noah kept staring at Emmanuel sprawled at his feet.

"We have to go," said Arielle softly.

"Yes," added Yvan. "My car is parked outside. Come on!"

"Your uncle is sure a take-charge kind of guy," Brutus said admiringly as he followed Yvan outside.

Noah and Arielle were alone.

"The dogs…" Noah gestured towards the door.

"I'll help you carry them. Let's go," said Arielle.

"Wait."

He reached into his coat pocket and pulled out Arielle's half-moon pendant.

"I put it in the manor safe last night so Nomis would see it in the morning. I went back to get it a few hours later because I knew you would need it tonight. That *we* would need it. Here, take it."

"Thank you," murmured Arielle. "You don't know how much this pendant means to me."

"Yes, I do," he replied.

Uncle Yvan stuck his head through the door.

"Hurry up! The Elves are almost here!"

Chapter 24

As they left the room, they could hear a faint screeching, like a congress of furious ravens.

"Sylphors!" exclaimed Brutus, looking upwards.

Noah stopped and searched the sky.

"They're flying," announced Noah.

Yvan and Brutus helped the two Valinn place the dogs on the back seat and cover them with a blanket.

"Will they be OK?" asked Arielle.

"I think so," Noah replied hopefully.

The screams were getting louder. *The Elves will be here soon,* thought Arielle. She had the impression they were circling overhead, like vultures around a carcass, and would soon swoop down to rip the flesh from their bones.

"Get in, quick!" urged Yvan as he got behind the wheel.

Brutus squeezed between Arielle and her uncle in the front seat. Noah grabbed a large canvas bag he had left outside room 23 before climbing into the back seat next to his dogs.

Once they were all aboard, Yvan sped across the parking lot and turned onto the street.

"Do you know how to use that?" Noah asked Brutus, pointing to the draugur sword in the Animalter's hand.

"Sleeping Ugly back at the motel seems to think so," said Brutus.

Arielle was still shaken from her close brush with death in the motel room. She kept thinking about Emmanuel and how twisted and cruel he had become. His eyes had been so different, so full of hate. The monster that attacked her may have looked human, but there had been nothing *human* about him. She had detected no trace of the boy she had known in the creature that had called itself Emmanuel.

And he was her brother! Arielle couldn't believe THAT either! What brother would treat his sister the way he had treated her? Uncle Yvan had also said that her parents had not been killed in a fire, as she had always been told. Was that story true? And if it weren't, would she be lucky enough to meet them one day?

"Are my parents still alive?" Arielle asked her uncle.

Yvan kept his eyes on the road.

"It's complicated, Arielle," he replied. "I don't think now is the best time to talk about it."

"I have to know!" she insisted. "You said that Emmanuel was my brother. Why did he attack me? And why was it necessary for me to be separated from my family?"

Yvan sat quietly for a few moments.

"The ability to host an Alter is passed from grandmother to granddaughter and from grandfather to grandson," he said, choosing his words carefully.

"I know that already."

"But you probably don't know that your grandmother also had the half-moon pendant and that her birthmark was white, like yours."

"Are you saying that my grandmother was a Valinn,

too?"

"There have been Valinn in every generation of Alters since the twelfth century," explained Yvan. "Your grandmother, Abigaël Queen, and Noah's grandfather, Mikael Davidoff, were the two Valinn of their time. The Elding Knight who gave the half-moon pendants to Noah was a friend of Mikael Davidoff's and had been ordered to give the pendants to the next generation of Valinn so that they could continue the legacy of their grandparents—the legacy of all the Queens and Davidoffs who had come before."

"So one member of each of our families is a Valinn, then," Noah remarked.

"Yes, until the prophecy is fulfilled and the Land of the Dead is liberated," said Yvan.

They sped through the night, aware that the Dark Elves would soon catch up to them. Arielle didn't care—she wanted answers!

"How do you know all this, Uncle Yvan?"

Again, Yvan paused before answering.

"Your mother, Gabrielle, told me. And your grandmother had told her. The Sylphors had found out that your mother was Abigaël's daughter. They knew that Gabrielle would give birth to the next generation of Valinn, so they had one of their Kobold servants seduce her."

Like Emmanuel tried to do to me. Arielle shivered at the thought.

"Your mother fell in love with this Kobold. Your parents' first child was a boy: Emmanuel. You came next," continued Yvan.

"What? My father's a *Kobold?*" Arielle was stunned.

"He's a Dark Elf, now. But he's only your father by chance. Your mother would have had a daughter—you—no matter which man she had been with."

"What's this Dark Elf's name?"

"Erik Saddington."

"*Saddington?*"

"Emmanuel's grandmother—she's your grandmother, too— is Erik's mother. Saddington is a powerful member of the caste of Sordes, a group of necromancers working with the Elves to defeat the Alters and conquer the world."

"You mean the Elves have a bunch of wizards helping them out?" exclaimed Brutus. "Man, just when I thought things couldn't get any worse!"

"What happened after I was born?" asked Arielle.

"Your father's mission was to take you from Gabrielle and hand you over to the Dark Elves. Your grandmother and Noah's grandfather had given their pendants to an Elding Knight. The Dark Elves knew the Knight would try to find you one day. They wanted to use you to lure him out of hiding in order to take the pendants. But your mother learned what the Dark Elves were up to and asked me to take care of you," said Yvan.

"Why didn't the Elves come after me?" asked Noah.

"You were being protected by the Alters. But they also wanted to use you to lure the Elding Knight into a trap."

"The Alters already know I'm the other Valinn?" Noah was dumbfounded.

"There's a reason Simon Vanesse is your best friend, kid," Yvan said.

Noah swore and slammed his fist onto his thigh in frustration.

"I thought I was so smart, that I had everyone fooled—but they were playing me all along. Nomis knew I wouldn't hurt you, Arielle, when he asked me to kill you the other night. Remember when Simon attacked you in the library yesterday? I bet his goal was really to make Emmanuel think the Alters were also looking for the pendants."

"Yes," agreed Yvan. "The Alters used the two of you as bait to lure the Elves into a trap. Thanks to Emmanuel, Falko learned that Arielle had one of the pendants, but he didn't know who had the other. But now he does, and he will do anything to get his hands on them. It is the only way he can defeat the Alters."

This is all my fault, Arielle berated herself silently. *Falko would never have found out that Noah is the other Valinn if I hadn't said anything to Emmanuel.*

"The Dark Elves won't stop hunting for us until we're dead!" exclaimed Noah.

"Your only chance is to seek shelter with the Alters. That is what Nomis and his grandfather Reivax have been hoping would happen. It is part of their plan," said Yvan.

"Are we going to Bombyx Manor?" asked Arielle. "With all those Elves on our tail?"

"Yes. Every Alter in town has gathered there for the occasion."

"We'll basically be serving up the Sylphors on a silver platter," observed Brutus.

"And believe me, the Alters are ready for them! The Alters also want to get the pendants, but their main goal is to destroy all of the Dark Elves from the New World Clans. This will buy them some time for them to regroup," Yvan licked his lips nervously.

"Reivax has been preparing for this day for the past forty years. When he opened the Saturnia factory in town, he convinced many Alters from across the country to settle in Glory and serve as his workforce. That's how the town was repopulated. This whole area is a massive Alter den. The raid on the manor two nights ago was only a setup; the Alters didn't put up much of a fight to make the Elves think there are fewer Alters than there really are. Reivax's plan worked. The Dark Elves are about to launch a massive attack on the Alters because they think their enemies are weak. One side will be wiped out tonight, but it won't be the Alters!"

"Why did you bring me to Glory if you knew this is where all the Alters live?" Arielle was puzzled.

"It was impossible to hide from the Elves and necromancers. They kept finding us, no matter where I went. So, I decided to cut a deal with the Alters and settle here. They promised that as long as the Elding Knight did not show up, they wouldn't make a move against you. Glory was the only place where the Dark Elves wouldn't dare go unless they weren't 100% sure both pendants were here."

"And tonight, thanks to us, you are going to lure the Elves to their deaths. Is that part of the deal you made with the Alters?" Arielle made no effort to mask her contempt for her uncle's intentions.

"That deal I made is what saved your life, Arielle. But after tonight, all bets are off. I don't think I can protect you and Noah any more once all of the Dark Elves have been eliminated. The Alters will do anything to capture the pendants."

"Uncle Yvan, is my mother still alive?"

"Arielle…"

She was annoyed at the way he kept avoiding the question.

"I want a straight answer! Is she alive: yes or no?"

"No," Yvan sighed.

"How did she die?"

"It doesn't matter."

"This is my *mother* we're talking about!" she shouted. "I think it's up to me to decide whether the way she died is important or not!"

"I can't say any more, Arielle. There's too much at

stake."

"What do you mean?"

"It'll all make sense soon."

Yvan rubbed his hand over his beard and stepped on the gas. Growling could be heard from the back seat. The DoberMen were waking up at last.

"How's it going, boys?" asked Noah.

Geri was the first to take human form.

"My head hurts," he complained.

"I think I'm going to be sick," added Freki.

"Poor babies," simpered Brutus. "That's what happens when you're a four-legged garbage can. Say, guys, how did E-manual the Kobold drug you? Did he toss you a couple of nice steaks stuffed full of sleeping pills or what?"

"Shut up, or I'll rip your head off," snarled Geri weakly.

"Oooh, I'm so scared. I nearly filled my litter box."

Arielle shot Brutus a look that meant, *One more word out of you, and you'll be dog chow.* Brutus took the hint and fell silent.

"Noah, do you have our clothes?"

The teenaged boy rummaged through the bag he had picked up at the motel and pulled out two sets of clothing that he gave to the DoberMen. He contemplated Arielle for a moment and reached back into the bag.

"I haven't forgotten about you," said Noah to Arielle, producing a woman's black blouse, pants, leather overcoat and boots.

"Hey, did you raid Neo's closet?" asked Brutus. "Mistress, you'll look like Trinity from *The Matrix* in those clothes. Rowwwr."

Arielle began to undress.

"There's a lady changing here, boys, so shut your eyes," said Brutus. He turned to Yvan. "But not you," Brutus added, pointing to the road. "You just keep doin' what you're doin'."

In a few moments, Arielle had squeezed into her Alter outfit.

"It's OK, everyone. I'm all dressed," she called out.

"Don't forget your accessories," Noah said, handing her a belt with a dozen acidus injectors attached to it.

There was a loud metallic thud. The car swerved sharply under the impact of an unknown force, but Yvan quickly regained control of the vehicle.

"What was that?" cried Brutus.

"Something hit us," said Yvan, gritting his teeth.

A second impact. A heavy object had slammed into the roof with enough force to dent it.

"Bloody Elves!" cursed Geri.

A volley of arrows embedded itself in the side of the car.

"They're trying to get us to slow down!" said Freki.

A third impact, the hardest one yet.

"Are they throwing themselves at the car?" asked Brutus scanning the darkness for their assailants.

"Exactly!" replied Yvan. "They're smashing into us one after the other. There's a huge flock of Elves chasing us!"

More arrows rained down upon the car.

"They're going to pop our tires!" yelled Freki.

The car careened to the right after the fourth impact.

Noah tapped Arielle on the shoulder.

"It's time to put on the pendant," he said.

She complied at once.

"Fra Retla! Fra Alter!"

Her transformation began the moment the pendant touched her skin. Her face became thinner, her hair grew longer and her freckles faded. The dark clothing fit her Alter form much more comfortably than her human one. Arielle felt supercharged with energy. Thanks to her newfound strength and agility, she was no longer afraid. Now she knew what Superman must feel like when he cast aside his persona of mild-mannered reporter Clark Kent. Bristling with confidence, she was ready to take on every pointy-eared demon on Earth.

Chapter 25

A Dark Elf landed on the trunk of the car.

He smashed the rear window with his fist and wriggled inside. The two DoberMen tackled him, but he struggled like a madman. Swiftly, Noah drew his draugur dagger and sliced off the Elf's right forearm. The Elf flailed about and howled—an awful, frightful keening that chilled the blood of the car's other occupants. Noah opened the door next to him, grabbed the maimed Sylphor by the jacket and threw him out of the speeding vehicle. The Elf bounced violently across the road and smashed into the guardrail.

"Whoa! He was quite a handful!" remarked Brutus.

"No kidding!" said Geri as he tossed the severed limb out the rear window.

Two other Sylphors appeared before the car, illuminated by the headlights. They landed on the hood, which groaned under their weight. Yvan soon ejected them with some skilful driving.

Shortly afterwards, a third Elf managed to grab onto

the windshield wipers. His body swung left and right as he fought to maintain his balance. Peering through the windshield, his eyes met Arielle's. He smiled lewdly at her, licking his lips in an obscene manner. Arielle snatched the sword out of Brutus's hands and plunged it through the windshield into the Sylphor's throat. *That* put an end to the horrible grinning. She waited until the evil gleam in his eyes faded before withdrawing the blade. With a gargling noise, the Elf released the wipers and slipped away into the darkness.

"You got him!" said Noah approvingly.

"I couldn't have done better myself," added Brutus with a sigh of relief.

The Elves continued to hurl themselves against the cars like kamikazes.

"Are we there yet?" asked Geri.

The were-dog's concern was justified. At this rate, they would never reach Bombyx Manor.

"Not far now!" replied Yvan as he swerved to the right to avoid two more Sylphors.

"I'm going to try to draw some of them off," said Noah. "I'll meet up with you at the manor!"

He climbed out of the rear window and flew into the sky.

"I'm going, too," said Arielle.

"No!" yelled Yvan. "We can't risk the Elves getting their hands on both pendants. You have to stay here!"

Arielle shook her head.

"I can't let Noah fight those demons alone!"

In a flash, she slipped into the back seat and crawled out the rear window.

The cold air helped Arielle focus her thoughts. She felt free—in mortal danger perhaps, but free nonetheless. She had a little trouble controlling her flight at first, but soon righted herself. Her coat acted like giant bird wings and helped lift her into the air. It seemed that a trace of Elleira remained—that Arielle had inherited her Alter's instincts and agility.

Glancing around, Arielle spotted Noah surrounded by over a dozen circling Sylphors wielding bows and draugur swords. Though the teenaged boy parried their attacks with ease, his foes would soon overcome him by weight of numbers. Drawing her weapon, she flew to his aid.

Arielle knew she would have to fight her way through the Elves to reach Noah. She swiftly decapitated one opponent and skewered a second. Six archers fired at this new threat, but Arielle dodged the arrows through a series of aerial tumbles that brought her near Noah.

"You're crazy! What are you doing here?" shouted Noah.

"Isn't it obvious?" replied Arielle. "I've come to help you!"

A Dark Elf charged them, but they quickly sliced him to ribbons.

"Were you worried about me?" he asked.

"Don't flatter yourself!" she snorted, bracing herself for the next onslaught.

Eight Sylphors hovered around Noah, and seven around Arielle. The teenaged girl countered blows from each of her assailants at a furious rate.

Between dodging two attacks, Arielle noticed that most of the Sylphors were still following her uncle's car as it headed for Bombyx Manor.

"Maybe we shouldn't have bothered coming out here," she said as the horde of Dark Elves disappeared in the distance.

"They aren't taking any chances," Noah answered.

The two Valinn remained back to back, repelling their foes' sword thrusts vigorously. Arielle was amazed at her combat skills. Her reflexes were so fast that she had trouble following her movements. The Elves she was fighting seemed to act with exaggerated slowness.

"Be careful not to lose control!" cautioned Noah. "Stay focused! You haven't mastered all of your Alter powers yet."

Arielle was having far too much fun to heed Noah's warning. Her swordplay was a blur of attacks, thrusts, feints and parries that overwhelmed her opponents.

"Arielle! Not so fast!" Noah shouted.

She beheaded two Elves in quick succession, and then reduced three others to powder with acidus injectors. Noah was enjoying similar success, his blade carving his opponents to pieces.

Arielle whittled her opposition down to two. The demons decided a joint attack was in their best interest, but Arielle was not worried. After all, a pair of Elves was no match for her Alter powers. She chopped the head off the first Elf and turned to face the second, who appeared more competent a warrior than his companion.

"This one's fast," she called to Noah as the Elf charged her with his draugur sword.

"He's caused you to break your stride! Land! I'll take care of him!" said Noah.

Arielle found it difficult to keep at bay this foe who was assailing her with increasingly powerful blows. She felt a sudden pain in her wrist that quickly shot up her arm all the way to her shoulder.

Noah defeated his remaining opponents. Only one Sylphor now remained, the one whose superior swordsmanship was getting the better of Arielle. Noah took up position next to her and tried to draw the Elf's attention, but the demon continued to press his attack on the girl, whose arm was now too numb to wield her weapon effectively. Her guard slowly dropped.

"Look out!" screamed Noah.

The Sylphor knocked Arielle's blade aside and punched her in the face, causing her sword to slip from her fingers and disappear into the darkness. The Elf hit her in the face a second time, stunning her. Unable to control her movements, she began to lose altitude. Her coat suddenly plastered itself to her body, preventing the wind from supporting her in mid-air.

Arielle hovered for a few seconds before beginning to fall. She was hazily aware of Noah lunging towards the Elf and stabbing him in the heart with an acidus injector. The Elf withered almost instantly.

The last thing she remembered before passing out was Noah speeding towards her…

ARIELLE opened her eyes and realized she was lying on the ground. Noah was bent over her still form.

"Nothing broken?" he asked, concerned.

The right side of her face ached.

"My jaw hurts and my arm feels a bit funny," she replied. "But apart from that, I think I'm OK. What happened?"

"Luckily, you fell from quite high up. I was able to catch you before you splattered all over the ground like a ripe melon."

Noah helped Arielle to her feet. The two of them were standing on the shoulder of Gleason Road, which led to Bombyx Manor and Crooked Lake. A forest was at their back.

"You're my hero," she said, massaging her jaw.

"Really?" Noah's eyes brightened.

"Really what?"

"You really think I'm your hero?"

The young girl's eyebrow shot up in surprise.

"It's just something you say. I didn't mean anything by it."

Her rescuer's face fell.

"Does that mean you're still not in love with me?" he said.

Arielle smiled, despite herself.

"No, not yet. Should I be?"

"I saved your life," Noah pointed out.

"It's only in fairy tales that the princess falls in love with the brave knight," she said. She was amused, more than anything, by this turn in their conversation. "In case you haven't noticed, our story sounds a lot more like a slasher movie."

Noah nodded sadly.

"Are you still in love with Simon?" he asked.

That question caught her off guard. *Was* she still in love with Simon? Had she ever been? It seemed such a long time ago that she wished Simon would take her in his arms...

"He isn't Simon anymore," she said. "He's Nomis."

"What did you see in Simon anyway?" Noah pressed the point.

"All kinds of things."

"Name one."

Arielle sighed.

"Noah, do you really think now is the best time to talk about this? Our friends are in danger."

"We can't do anything until they reach the manor, otherwise the Elves will become suspicious. That gives us a few minutes to talk," he said.

Noah was right. The Sylphors had to continue to believe the two half-moon pendants were in the car, which was serving as the bait to draw them to the manor and into the Alters' trap.

"So?" Noah insisted. "Why Simon?"

Arielle thought back to the grade-school incident with Richard and the dodgeball game.

"You'll think it's silly."

"Try me."

"In the fourth grade, Richard was making fun of me, and Simon put him in his place," she began. "Do you remember how I was always picked last for teams in gym class? One day, Richard said in front of everyone that I was too lousy a player to be on his team. Simon told him to leave me alone. That was the first time a boy stood up for me. I think that was when I fell in love with him."

"Hmm, cute story," said Noah.

"It was puppy love," Arielle rolled her eyes. "I was just a kid and didn't know much about love back then."

"Do you know much about love now?"

She laughed.

"Not really."

Noah drew his finger along the scar on his face.

"Do you think I'm ugly?" he asked.

Disarmed by this question, Arielle remained speechless. She had no idea his scar bothered him so much.

"No, I don't," she said after a few seconds. "Honestly, I think it makes you kind of cute, in a roguish sort of way."

"You're a good liar, Venus. But thanks anyway," he smiled at her, and then glanced at his watch. "I think we should go now. Your uncle and the Animalters will need our help when the Alters and Sylphors realize we aren't in the car."

Before Noah could launch himself into the air, Arielle gave him a peck on the cheek.

"Whoa! What do I have to do to get another kiss?" said Noah.

Arielle smiled.

"Ummmm—save my life again?"

"No problem!"
A strong wind rose and caused their coats to billow out. Together, they flew into the night sky.

Chapter 26

The distinctive silhouette that gave Crooked Lake its name quickly became visible in the distance…

Arielle and Noah skimmed the treetops to avoid detection. Thanks to their night vision, they could see Yvan's car racing down Gleason Road with a horde of Dark Elves trailing behind. It looked like a murder of crows swarming a small wounded animal.

"They're almost at the manor!" he yelled to make himself heard over the wind. "Ready?"

"Do you have a plan?" asked Arielle.

"The Elves are going to realize they've been had. You can bet they won't go down without a fight. We'll have to wait until the Elves and Alters begin to kill each other. Then we sneak in, rescue our friends and sneak out. Let's go!"

Noah surged forward, quickly outdistancing Arielle. She managed to increase her speed by force of will and caught up to him.

"There!" said Noah, pointing to the manor's multi-car garage. "That's a good place to land. No-one will see us."

They reached their hiding spot just as Yvan's car

sped up the lane, which was lined with towering maple trees. The car crossed the wide esplanade and screeched to a halt near the marble staircase leading up to the terrace and the manor's front door. The Elves landed, positioning themselves around the vehicle to block every escape route. From their vantage point, Noah and Arielle could see and hear everything that was happening in the esplanade.

One of the Elves sauntered towards the car. Arielle identified him at once: it was Falko. Dressed in worn boots, a ratty coat and grungy shirt, he looked more like some squeegee kid than one of the most dangerous Sylphors on the continent.

Falko yanked the driver's side door off and tossed it almost all the way to the trees like it weighed nothing.

"Get out!" ordered Falko.

Uncle Yvan climbed out first, followed by Brutus and the DoberMen.

"Which of you has the pendants?" Falko thundered.

"The Valinn do," replied Brutus, "but they're not here right now. If you would like to leave a message after the beep…"

Falko struck the were-cat viciously, knocking him to the ground. The Voivod then drew his draugur sword and held it to Yvan's throat.

"So, tell me where I can find your 'niece'!" he snarled.

"I wouldn't know where to look," answered Yvan.

"You're lying!"

"Of course, he's lying," said a voice from the terrace. It was Nomis, who was standing on the terrace holding a glowing sword. He was flanked by his raven Animalter and the Alter of Lea Darling.

"Watch out for Ael," whispered Noah. "She is very dangerous. Nomis chose her to be his personal bodyguard for a reason."

Falko lowered his blade—much to Arielle's relief—and took a few steps towards the terrace.

"Stay out of this!" shouted Falko to Nomis. "This is Dark Elf business!"

"Actually," countered Nomis, "you and your little band of pixies are here tonight because the Alters made a deal with Arielle's uncle."

Falko burst out laughing.

"What? Do you mean to tell me that this is a set-up and that dear Uncle Yvan meant to lure us all here?"

Nomis nodded. That was the prearranged signal for the other Alters to come out of their hiding places across the estate. Most of them had been camouflaging themselves in the thickets surrounding the esplanade. Among their number, Arielle recognized the CeeCees and Simon's friends Oliver Guinness and William Louis-Seize. Every Alter was armed with a draugur weapon. They circled the Elves, who did not seem to be taking this threat seriously.

Falko continued, as arrogant as ever.

"I thought you had learned your lesson when we crashed your party the other night. You kids are out of your league. You should stick to dressing up in black leather and playing with your pets. You don't scare anybody."

"We brought reinforcements this time," said Nomis.

A grey-bearded man exited the manor and strode across the terrace to stand next to the young Alter.

"Old Xavier Vanesse," mocked Falko. "He's your reinforcements? You must really be desperate."

Nomis's grandfather responded in a booming voice.

"I am Reivax, the Alter of Xavier Vanesse. You're right, Falko. The young Alters could never defeat you. But, if their grandparents decided to get involved..."

On cue, a second group of Alters came out of hiding.

They were considerably older and had grey hair.

"Would you look at that?" chuckled the Voivod. "You emptied the old age home for this little party! Is it bingo night already?"

Arielle couldn't believe her eyes! Among the new arrivals were Hellgebra, her math teacher; Mr. Gravel, her history teacher; Mr. Gordon, her English teacher; as well as nearly two dozen familiar faces, including her school bus driver, one of the clerks from the grocery store, the mailman and the old cobbler. The others were all retirees from the Saturnia factory who generally spent their days at diners or at the park. She had only ever known them as a group of tired and flabby seniors, but in their Alter forms, they were strong and noble warriors.

"We have to get my uncle and the Animalters out of there!" whispered Arielle urgently. "If they are stuck in the middle when the fighting starts, they'll be massacred!"

"You're right!" agreed Noah. "But we can't show ourselves now. It would be too risky."

Falko's smugness vanished. He and many of the Elves had sized up the opposition and realized that they were outnumbered by at least three-to-one with the arrival of the second wave of Alters.

Reivax addressed the Voivod a second time.

"My plan had always been to lay the greatest Sylphor trap in history. I founded the Saturnia plant as an excuse to get hundreds of Alters to settle here in Glory. I have been planning tonight's battle for over forty years. You Elves are so stupid! I knew you would walk right into my trap—a trap that is about to snap shut on your necks. Tonight, we are going to crush you for turning your backs on our masters, Loki and Hel!"

"Enough with the speeches, old man! Come down here and fight!" roared Falko.

A hint of a smile appeared on Reivax's face.

"I have been waiting a long time for you to say that," replied the Alter before leaping down from the terrace.

"Death to the Elves!" bellowed Nomis and Ael, following in turn.

The remaining Alters charged towards their foes, most on foot, while others took to the air to prevent any Sylphors from flying away. The enemy forces clashed in the centre of the esplanade in a flurry of warcries, arrows and slashing blades. Within moments of the battle being joined, many had fallen, headless, since decapitation was the surest method of killing a Sylphor or an Alter.

"Ready?" Noah glanced at the other Valinn.

Arielle nodded, tightening her grip on the pommel of her sword.

"Then let's roll!" he said.

The two Valinn burst out of their hiding spot behind the garage and quickly reached the esplanade. They plunged into the melee, wielding their draugur swords and acidus injectors with deadly precision as they frayed a path through the Alters and Elves to reach Yvan's car.

"Where are they?" asked Noah.

Arielle glanced inside the car. It was empty. Out of the corner of her eye, she spotted Geri and Freki near the marble staircase, where they were fending off a half-dozen Alters. A little way to the left, Arielle watched as Brutus thrust an acidus injector into the chest of two Elves. The Animalter then snatched up their draugur swords and handed one to Yvan, who was standing next to him. Two other Elves appeared, bearing down on them.

"I'll help Geri and Freki!" cried Noah, cutting the head off the Elf attacking him. "You give your uncle and Brutus a hand. We'll meet up at the entrance to the gardens!"

"OK!" replied the girl, dodging an Alter's wild swings.

Noah knocked her assailant unconscious with a punch to the jaw before leaping over to the DoberMen. Arielle fought her way through the combatants to reach Brutus and Yvan, who were defending themselves fiercely. Arielle was impressed by her uncle's swordplay.

"Glad to see you, Mistress," panted Brutus. "As you can see, we got our hands full out here."

"I noticed," she replied.

"How are you?" asked Yvan. "Are you and Noah all right?"

"We're fine. Sorry it took so long to get here."

Yvan's swirling blade cut down, in quick succession, a Dark Elf, an Alter and another Dark Elf.

"Where did you learn to fight like that?" Arielle stared at her uncle in amazement.

"In university. I was a champion fencer."

Scanning the crowd, Arielle saw Noah near the main staircase. He and the DoberMen were heading towards the path along the manor's western wing that led to the back gardens.

"This way! Hurry!" said Arielle as she motioned to her uncle and Brutus to follow her.

More opponents leaped at the trio, but they were soon dispatched. Arielle, Brutus and Yvan set off at once. A volley of arrows whistled overhead as they ran towards the path Noah and the DoberMen had just taken. Behind them, Elves and Alters continued to slaughter one another with arrow and draugur blade.

Arielle glanced over her shoulder at the fighting: it was almost over. The Alters' greater numbers gave them the upper hand. Arielle knew that she and her friends would have to leave the manor before the Alters claimed victory; otherwise, she and Noah would be pitted against Nomis and Reivax. The Alters knew that the Valinn had the half-moon pendants. The bait for tonight's trap would then become the prey.

The three of them finally joined Noah and the DoberMen.

"Is anyone hurt?" asked Noah. Fortunately, their injuries were minor, just a few cuts and bruises. The six of them hurried down the path to the rear gardens.

"You've had your fun!" said a man's voice from nearby. "But playtime's over."

Spinning around, they saw Nomis and Ael sauntering over to them from the other side of a large pond, in the centre of which stood a beautiful fountain shaped like a butterfly.

"Give us the pendants!" Ael called out.

"Come and get them!" replied Noah.

Ael and Nomis exchanged looks and burst out laughing.

"Noah, old buddy," said Nomis, drawing his sword. "You're as brave as ever. Too bad you've chosen the wrong side."

"No!" Noah pointed his weapon at the approaching Alters. "I have always chosen the right side, just like all of my ancestors did before me!"

Arielle, her uncle and the Animalters readied themselves for battle once more. Before the two sides could cross swords, however, a pair of Sylphors swooped down from the sky towards Nomis and Ael. The latter tried to fend off her attacker, but a powerful blow sent her crumpling to the ground. The larger Elf seized Nomis by the throat and lifted him into the air.

"I will not let the pendants slip through my fingers again!" roared the Dark Elf.

Arielle gasped; the Elf was Falko. His display of strength was both terrifying and intimidating.

"You have underestimated me for the last time!" gloated Falko before stabbing the young Alter through the heart with his draugur sword. Nomis twitched for a few seconds—and was still. The instant Nomis drew his last breath, he reverted to his Dayform. Falko was now holding the impaled body of Simon Vanesse in one hand. Smiling cruelly, the Voivod withdrew his weapon, letting the teenager's corpse fall to the ground.

"Get the pendants!" Falko ordered the other Sylphor.

"Yes, Master," the Sylphor responded.

As the second Elf approached, Arielle studied him carefully. That voice, that walk…

"Emmanuel?" she said.

The young Elf's eyes were now as black as Falko's.

"My name is Mastermyrr!" he said proudly. "I have been elevated. Emmanuel is dead. I am now the latest in a long line of Voivods."

Mastermyrr stared at Arielle. His head was shaven, his ears long and pointy, and his skin as pale as that of any Sylphor. He looked like a cadaver.

"They turned you into a monster," said Arielle, choking back tears.

Emmanuel gloated. "It's what I've always wanted!"

Arielle shook her head in disgust. "Why did you do the things you did? Why did you want to hurt me so badly?"

"Because that's what I do, Arielle, I hurt people. Just like our father does. Isn't that right, dad?" Emmanuel kept his eyes locked on his sister as he spoke.

Arielle whipped around to look at Yvan, her mouth agape. *Was Emmanuel referring to Uncle Yvan?!*

"You're absolutely right, son," said a deep male voice.

But Yvan's lips had not moved. It was Falko who had spoken.

CHAPTER 27

Falko walked towards Arielle and her friends.

"I know I look too young to be your father," said Falko, "but I had just turned twenty-five when the previous Voivod elevated me. I have looked this way ever since. It would be stupid of me to complain, don't you think? Women love my smooth Elven skin."

Stunned, Arielle took a step backwards. She couldn't believe this young skinhead was her father.

"I went by the name Erik Saddington when I met your mother. I loved her very much. She was gorgeous. Many other men wanted her, but she chose me. I suppose there was something about me she couldn't resist. Kobold servants can be pretty charming when they need to be." He glanced at Emmanuel. "But I guess you already know that, right?"

Emmanuel smirked, and Arielle shuddered.

Ignoring his children's reactions, Falko went on. "For a time, your mother and I were very happy. But then Romeo here showed up," he pointed to Yvan, "and weaseled himself into our lives. I never knew if Gabrielle and he were lovers or just friends. But it doesn't matter anymore. Becoming a Sylphor has freed me, like it has freed Emmanuel. Love and jealousy are only feelings that a mortal has. It has been many years since I have thought about getting revenge. There is only one thing that I want now."

"The half-moon pendants," Noah said.

"Gold star for you, kid!" said Falko.

"Is my mother still alive?" asked Arielle.

The Voivod seemed surprised.

"What? You mean your 'uncle' never told you?"

"That's enough, Erik!" growled Yvan.

"You never told her that her mother died—and that you're the one who killed her?" said Falko.

"Shut up, demon!"

"You let her be burned alive!" Falko crowed.

Arielle's eyes pleaded with her uncle, *Please tell me that's not true!*

"We were trying to escape in Gabrielle's car," said Yvan. "The Dark Elves figured out we were trying to hide one of the Valinn from them. They chased us clear across the city and into the countryside. They took turns smashing into the car, like they did tonight. I lost control of the car. We crashed." Yvan hesitated before continuing. "I didn't have time to save her, Arielle."

Now she understood why her uncle had not wanted to tell her anything about her mother.

"The Elves were coming," Yvan said. "I had to get you away from them as quickly as I could. To protect you."

Falko took a step towards the girl.

"Your mother sacrificed her life so that you could live," he said. "Don't you think that was a heavy price to pay?"

Arielle did not care whether Falko was her father or not. All she wanted to do was slit his throat with her draugur sword.

"Everything is your fault!" she accused him. "You and the Elves are the ones who killed my mother. You're the ones who made the car crash!"

A screech pierced the night—the hunting cry of an animal swooping to the attack. Glancing upwards, Arielle spotted Nomis's raven Animalter plunging towards Falko, its beak open and eyes burning with hatred.

The Sylphor easily dodged the raven's first pass, but the wily bird quickly circled its opponent to flank him. Falko was unable to dodge a second time, and the raven's claws dug deeply into Falko's face. Emmanuel sprang to his father's aid, but the bird kept tearing at Falko's flesh as it hammered on his bald head with its beak. Emmanuel finally managed to grip the Animalter and made it let go. The raven squirmed free and flew away into the night.

"Damn Animalters!" cursed Falko, wiping the blood off his face with his coat sleeve. His face was a gory mess. "But don't worry about me!" he added. "We Elves heal pretty fast. I just need a few leaves to patch myself up!"

It took those standing near the pond a few seconds to notice that the raven Animalter was not alone. Dozens of Alters had arrived on the scene, lead by Reivax.

"It's over, Falko!" thundered the old Alter. "You lost! Your best warriors were slaughtered. The only two Elves left are you and that puny runt."

At that instant, Reivax spotted Simon's lifeless body lying in the dirt.

"Monster! You killed my heir!" His face twisted with anguish. "My grandson!"

Falko laughed coldly.

"What do I care?"

The Sylphor's insolence only stoked the old Alter's rage. Reivax ordered his forces to draw their weapons and chop Falko to pieces. A horde of enraged Alters swarmed the Voivod.

"I think that's our cue to leave," Noah whispered to Arielle and Brutus.

"Yeah," agreed Brutus. "I don't feel like watching that guy get sliced and diced."

Noah gestured to Yvan and the DoberMen; the three nodded in acknowledgement. The six friends slowly backed towards the forest. They had almost reached the edge of the estate when an Alter's voice rang out.

"Hey! Stop!"

"They spotted us!" exclaimed Geri.

"The Valinn are over there!" yelled a second Alter. "They have the pendants! Get them!"

"Quick! Into the woods!" barked Noah. "It's our only chance!"

They dashed through the forest along a trail that was so narrow, they could only travel in single file. Loud cries echoed behind them as the Alters launched into pursuit. Arielle was sure they would be captured soon.

"We have to split up so the Alters can't get both pendants," said Yvan when they got to a fork in the trail. "I'll go with Arielle and Brutus down this path. Noah and the DoberMen will take the other. We'll meet up at Gleason Road."

"OK," said Noah. "But don't take any unnecessary risks. And no flying. They would spot us right away."

"Let's go! They're coming!" urged Yvan.

Brutus, Arielle and Yvan hurried down the right-hand trail, while Noah and his Animalters took the left.

The forest was pitch black. Unlike Arielle and Brutus, Yvan did not have night vision. His niece had to lead him down the trail by the hand, which made for very slow progress. Too slow, in fact—the Alters were gaining on them.

"Go on without me," Yvan said after stumbling through the dark for about a minute. "Gleason Road can't be far now. Move!"

Yvan drew his sword and positioned himself to block the Alters' advance. The sword cast a pale glow that allowed him to see a little.

"I'll hold them off as long as I can," he said bravely.

"I'll stay with you," offered Arielle, grabbing the pommel of her weapon.

"No. Everything depends on you, Arielle. You have to go!"

"I can't just leave you!" she exclaimed.

Arielle realized that she didn't know her uncle well at all. Never would she have imagined him capable of making such a sacrifice. She had always thought he did not care about her, but she had been proven wrong about him several times this night.

"Get her out of here!" Yvan ordered Brutus.

"He's right!" said Brutus as he dragged Arielle away. "There's no time to lose! Think of the pendant!"

Arielle gave in. She and the Animalter sprinted down the trail.

"I can hear them getting closer," Brutus said. He stopped running. "Your uncle didn't slow them down much. It's my turn to try."

"No!" yelled Arielle. "We're almost at the road. We can both make it!"

"The Animalter's handbook states that an Animalter must know when to sacrifice himself to save his master. I believe that time has come."

"No!"

Brutus drew his sword, as Yvan had done not long before. The eerie blue light illuminated the Animalter's large feline head.

"Thanks for letting me sleep at the foot of your bed for all those years, Mistress," he said.

He nodded in farewell, and charged towards the

approaching Alters bellowing, "Look out! This puss is gonna kick some booty!"

Arielle hesitated as she watched his retreating form, and then turned and ran towards the road.

The pendant, girl, think of the pendant.

She charged straight ahead, trying to convince herself that she was doing the right thing. But nothing could stop the tears from pouring down her cheeks.

Behind her, along the trail, she had abandoned the only family she had ever known.

CHAPTER 28

Fueled by her grief, Arielle raced onwards, keeping her eyes focused straight ahead.

Arielle felt vulnerable and alone. In the darkness, the trees looked ominous. She had the impression that they would reach down and grab her with their branches, holding her until the Alters arrived. She wished that Uncle Yvan, Brutus and Noah were there, or that Elleira was still alive to give her advice.

The sounds of pursuit stopped. Brutus and her uncle must have succeeded in delaying the Alters after all. But at what cost? Were they still alive or had they been killed? She desperately wanted to see them both again.

Arielle noticed a dim light through the trees and was certain she had almost reached Gleason Road. She hoped that Noah and the DoberMen would meet up with her soon.

The teenaged girl finally got to the edge of the forest. Glancing around, she did not see any sign of Noah or the dogs. The light she had spotted earlier was actually the headlights of a vehicle driving up the road towards the manor. Arielle leaped out of her hiding spot. Maybe she could convince the driver to turn around and drive her back to town.

Arielle stood in the middle of the road waving her arms. The vehicle skidded to a halt right in front of her. Arielle recognized the old minivan: it was the one that belonged to Elizabeth's father.

"Arielle, is that you?"

It took her a few seconds to realize that Elizabeth was at the wheel.

"What are you doing here?" Arielle asked incredulously.

"Get in, quick!" said Elizabeth. "I'll explain on the way back to town!"

Arielle hurried over to the passenger's side and opened the door. As she was about to climb into the minivan, she remembered what Elizabeth had told her that afternoon about Elliot having to take his stepfather's last name when his mother remarried.

"But Eli wasn't E.Q.," mumbled Arielle, and she started backing towards the forest.

"Where are you going?" shouted Elizabeth. "Come back!"

The Valinn drew her draugur sword.

"You lied to me," said Arielle. "You had me believe that Eli had changed his last name to make me suspect him and not Emmanuel."

"What are you talking about?" Elizabeth replied, getting out of the minivan and walking towards her friend.

"Don't come any closer!" yelled Arielle. "You're working with the Elves! That explains why you just showed up here in the middle of the night. You were going to Bombyx Manor to help your new friends, weren't you?"

"You're being paranoid."

Maybe I am, Arielle thought, *but after everything that happened tonight, no-one could blame me.*

Elizabeth continued to walk towards Arielle.

"I want proof that they haven't turned you into a Kobold. Show me your wrists!" Arielle ordered Elizabeth. "And lift up your hair! I want to see the back of your neck, too!"

"But Arielle, I'm telling you it's just me," the other girl sounded peeved.

Someone opened the side door of the minivan. A face peered out slowly, like it was emerging from a void. It was Saddington. The old sorceress must have hidden herself in the back seat when she had seen Arielle in the road, and then told Elizabeth to lure her into the minivan. Saddington would have then been able to deal with Arielle by casting a spell on her or forcing her to drink a potion. The young Alter was relieved she had avoided falling into their trap.

"What are you waiting for?" shrieked Saddington. "Get that sword away from her and bring her here!"

"Yes, Mistress," replied Elizabeth. Suddenly, her gaze hardened behind the round frames of her glasses, and her smile twisted into a horrible grin. She made a weird growling noise.

"Do you really want to hurt me, Elizabeth? I'm your best friend," said Arielle soothingly.

The normally gentle and trusting look on Elizabeth's face had been replaced by a hideous mask of viciousness and hate.

"My masters told me to hurt you," she hissed, "and I always obey."

There was no longer anything human about Elizabeth. The Elves had transformed her into a monster whose fingers were curved like talons. As Arielle was backing away from her friend, she bumped into something solid.

"Leaving so soon? But I just got here," said a voice from behind her.

Before Arielle could react, a powerful hand snatched her draugur sword away. She spun around to face her opponent: it was Emmanuel. He seized her arms and held her fast. As she struggled vainly, he dragged her towards him and pressed his cold lips against hers.

"Alters may be more agile, but Sylphors are much stronger," gloated Emmanuel after their kiss.

He squeezed Arielle's arms tightly, his fingers digging into her flesh.

"Ow! Let me go, Emmanuel!" she cried.

"My name is Mastermyrr!" he corrected her.

Releasing Arielle's arms, he quickly pulled the half-moon pendant over her head, which caused her to immediately revert to her Dayform. Without the pendant, she was powerless.

"Where is Falko?" Saddington asked her grandson.

"He's dead," replied the Dark Elf, stuffing the pendant into his coat pocket. "Reivax and his Alters massacred him. I got away by the skin of my teeth."

"The Voivod is dead! Long live the Voivod!" said the witch.

"What are you so happy for? You just found out your son died!" Arielle was shocked by Saddington's lack of compassion. With a heart that cold, the teenager thought the old woman must have ice water flowing through her veins.

"Erik died for our cause," said Saddington. "I am proud of his sacrifice."

Turning to Emmanuel, she continued.

"Mastermyrr, you are now the head of the New World Clans. Are you ready to guide the Sylphors to victory? They need a strong leader."

"There is no-one left to lead," he replied. "The New

World Clans have been wiped out by the Alters. I'm the only survivor."

"The Old World Voivods will soon send reinforcements," Saddington assured him. "Do you have the pendant?"

Emmanuel nodded.

"Perfect!" said the witch. "There's no need to go all the way to the manor anymore. Let's go home at once."

Elizabeth and Emmanuel dragged Arielle into the minivan and shoved her roughly inside. Emmanuel climbed in next and slammed the side door shut behind him. He then grabbed Arielle's arm and forced her to the seat in the very back. He sat down beside her, intent on watching her every move. In the meantime, Saddington got behind the wheel, while Elizabeth climbed into the passenger seat next to the sorceress.

"What do you need me for?" Arielle was confused as to why she was being held hostage.

"To lure your boyfriend into a trap," answered Saddington. "Noah will try to rescue you the minute he finds out we are keeping you prisoner. And when he does, we will take his pendant. After all, we do need both pendants to destroy every Alter on Earth."

"Noah is too smart to fall for your tricks!" Arielle's tone was defiant.

Saddington cackled.

"Love can blind even the bravest of warriors, my dear."

"I spotted Noah and his dogs fighting some Alters in a clearing as I flew through the trees," said Emmanuel. "It looked like he was winning."

"I'm sure Noah is a resourceful young man," added Saddington. "He'll find a way to escape."

The old woman then addressed her grandson.

"Mastermyrr, it's time to leave the clue."

The Elf drew out one of his leather bracelets with

the owl stud motif from his coat pocket. Arielle instantly recognized the bracelet, and she knew that Saddington and Emmanuel expected that Noah would, too.

Emmanuel handed the bracelet to Elizabeth. The girl lowered the window and threw the bracelet into the ditch by the side of the road, where the DoberMen were sure to find it with their keen sense of smell.

Chapter 29

"Do you remember our mother?" Arielle asked Emmanuel. The lights of the town were now visible in the distance.

The young man did not answer.

"I don't remember her at all," she added.

"Be quiet back there!" ordered Saddington, casting a dark look over her shoulder at her prisoner. Arielle held her gaze until the old woman turned around.

"Our father lied, Emmanuel," whispered Arielle. "Saddington, too. They were the ones who made you do bad things."

"What do you want, little sister? For me to feel sorry or guilty? I told you already: I'm rotten to the core—and proud of it."

"It's never too late to do the right thing," she said.

"It's too late for him," croaked Saddington. "He did what he had to do. And now, he is free."

"I don't believe you!" the young girl shot back.

"Enough talking! Mastermyrr, make her shut up!" ordered the sorceress.

Emmanuel balled a fist and prepared to strike Arielle,

but held back at the last second.

"I thought Dark Elves could feel no emotion," Arielle said as she looked him deep in the eyes. He was hesitating—she could sense it. Unfortunately for her, he made up his mind very fast.

"Thanks for reminding me!" snarled Emmanuel.

He punched Arielle hard in the face. Her head whipped back and smashed into the window frame.

She collapsed onto the seat, unconscious.

"ARIELLE! HEY, ARIELLE!"

Someone was calling out to her.

"Arielle, wake up!"

The young girl groggily opened her eyes. She was sitting on the floor in a dark and damp room, with her hands tied behind her to a pipe. She opened and closed her mouth to lessen the ache in her sore cheek.

"Are you all right?"

As her eyes adapted to the dim light, she studied her surroundings. The room looked like a basement. The moonlight filtering through a tiny, hastily-boarded window was the only source of illumination.

"Who's there?" she called out.

"It's me, Elliot," replied the voice.

Arielle focused her eyes and saw a figure sitting along the opposite wall. She could barely make out the face— her fellow prisoner was Elliot! He, too, was tied to a pipe.

"I thought..." she began, then paused. Her cheek was killing her. "I thought you were dead."

"Emmanuel was going to kill me if I didn't give him my clothes, so I figured, '*It's either my pants or my life.*' And then he tied me up."

"Did Emmanuel take your Nikes, too?"

"Yeah. Rose is going to kill me when she finds out."

Arielle felt the room spinning. She was worried that she would pass out again.

"What's going to happen to us, Arielle?" asked Elliot.

The teenaged girl had no idea. The only thing she knew for certain was that Noah would be there soon. She had to find a way to warn him before he fell into Saddington's trap.

"I think Elizabeth is on their side," continued Elliot. "I didn't see her, but I heard her talking to Emmanuel and the old bat."

"I know," said Arielle. "Do you think you could get free?"

"I've been trying to wiggle a hand loose all day," he said. "I think it's working, kind of."

"Keep at it."

They heard footsteps overhead. Arielle was positive it was Noah. She had the strangest impression she could sense his presence.

"Who's up there?" Elliot wondered aloud.

"Eli, how long was I out for?"

"About an hour," answered the young man as he struggled to get free.

"An hour?"

Noah and the dogs would have had plenty of time to escape from the Alters and find Emmanuel's bracelet, thought Arielle. *The dogs would then smell my scent—and Emmanuel's—near where the bracelet was lying in the ditch. Noah would figure out that I had been captured by Emmanuel and Saddington, and was most likely being held at their house. He would probably come right here to rescue me.*

"Get out of here, Noah!" Arielle screamed as loudly as she could.

She tried once more to wriggle out of her bonds, but no luck. The harder she pulled on the rope, the more it tightened around her wrists. With her Alter-enhanced strength, she could have snapped the rope. But since her enemies currently had her pendant...

"Noah, it's a trap! You have to get out of here now!" yelled Arielle.

Elliot gaped at her.

"You're crazy! Noah, don't listen to her!" Elliot shouted in turn. "Come back here! We're both in the basement!"

"Don't say that, Eli!" Arielle pleaded. "He'll be killed if he doesn't get out of this house right away!"

"Sorry, Arielle," retorted her fellow prisoner. "But I don't really feel like ending up as some ingredient in the old witch's cauldron. NOAH! DOWN HERE!"

The two captives looked up as a door opened. Light shone through the door, illuminating the basement stairs.

"Arielle?"

The voice was definitely that of Noah Davidoff.

"It's a trap! Run!" Arielle shrieked at the top of her lungs.

A second later, Noah bounded down the stairs three at a time and hurried towards her.

"Are you all right?" he asked, hugging her.

"They're using me as bait to capture you," she said.

"I know."

"You know? And you came anyway?"

"Do you really think I would abandon you?"

Arielle smiled at him.

"The Alters captured Geri and Freki after we found the bracelet," said Noah as he examined the wound on Arielle's cheek. "I heard them say they had your uncle and Brutus, too."

Relieved, Arielle's smile grew wider. She was determined to rescue her friends the minute she was free.

As Noah reached over to snap her bonds, there was a dazzling flash in the basement. Saddington appeared in the centre of a globe of light, which surrounded her small, hunched form like an aura.

The magician extended a hand towards Noah and spoke words of power, "*Erino kaltebar onima!*" A ball of fire flew from her hand and struck Noah, flinging him into the cement wall. He fell to the ground, stunned.

Arielle looked on helplessly, still tied firmly to the pipe.

Noah rose slowly to his feet. Saddington immediately fired another ball of fire at the young man, sending him smashing into the wall once more. Unbeaten, he got up a second time.

"Stop it! You'll kill him!" cried Arielle.

Saddington laughed.

"So what?"

The aura of the old sorceress grew brighter and swallowed her. She vanished, only to re-appear an instant later next to Noah. He made to draw his sword, but Saddington was faster, quickly casting a spell that paralyzed the teenager. Noah looked like he had been frozen in time, with his hand about to grasp the pommel of his sword. Only his eyes could still move. They searched the room in a panic, but stopped when his gaze met Arielle's.

The light bulb in the ceiling blinked on. Emmanuel and Elizabeth came slowly down the stairs, crossed the basement and positioned themselves on either side of the old woman. Emmanuel pulled something out of his coat pocket and handed it to his grandmother: Arielle's half-moon pendant.

"The Alters thought they could get their hands on the pendants before we could!" crowed Saddington as she claimed her prize. "What a bunch of idiots! Reivax needed forty years to come up with his plan! But it only took Mastermyrr and me six months to come up with ours."

Emmanuel drew his draugur sword and stood before Noah.

"Should I cut off his head or stab him through the heart?" he asked the witch, waving his sword in Noah's face.

"Do what you want," she answered, "as long as Noah stops being a problem."

Emmanuel nodded.

"Don't do it!" begged Arielle. "You're not a murderer—I see it in your eyes! There's a part of you that's still human!"

"No," responded Emmanuel without looking at her. "I already told you that Emmanuel is dead. My name is Mastermyrr."

The Elf pulled his sword back...

"Emmanuel, NO!!!"

...and plunged it into Noah's chest.

Chapter 30

"NOOOOOOOOOOOOOOOOOOOO!" Arielle howled in anguish.

Emmanuel inserted the sword all the way to the hilt into Noah's torso before pulling it out. The blade was coated in blood. Still paralyzed by Saddington's spell, Noah did not react. But Arielle could see the agony and despair in the eyes of a young man about to die in silence, and alone...

Emmanuel took a step towards Noah and ripped off his pendant.

"Elves 2, Alters 0!" cackled the aged sorceress. Noah made a strange wheezing sound before changing back to his Dayform. Without his pendant, he could not keep his Alter powers. Noah kept his eyes locked on Arielle throughout his ordeal.

"Noah," she murmured, tears welling in her eyes, "I'm here..."

He acknowledged her with a look and shut his eyes.

"Please, don't go," Arielle pleaded, "not yet."

Arielle could see he was still breathing, but that brought her little comfort. She burst into tears.

"You monsters!" she sobbed angrily.

Emmanuel sheathed his weapon and walked over to his grandmother to give her the other pendant. The old woman marvelled at the two pieces of jewellery in her knotty fingers.

"So small, yet so powerful," she said in awe.

Taking a pendant in each hand, she held them over her head. In a solemn tone, she said, "I, Hezadel Saddington, invoke the power of the half moons!"

She began to bring the pendants together.

"May your union banish the Alters from Midgard forever!"

Suddenly, Elizabeth sprang into action. Her fists clenched, she pounced on the witch and knocked her down.

"You old hag!" Elizabeth spit out the words as she pummelled the sorceress, who had dropped the pendants to protect herself. Emmanuel quickly scooped up one pendant, but Elizabeth snatched the second before he could get it. She dodged to one side and leaped over to Arielle. Kneeling before her friend, Elizabeth placed the pendant around Arielle's neck.

"Forgive me," said Elizabeth.

Arielle felt the warmth of the pendant on her skin, which quickly spread throughout her body. Shutting her eyes, she spoke the command words engraved on the pendant, "Fra Retla! Fra Alter!"

The transformation began immediately. Arielle could feel her senses grow keener and her strength increase as she underwent her Altermorphosis. Her outfit once again fit properly.

Arielle opened her eyes to see Emmanuel charge towards her, but Elizabeth bravely placed herself between Arielle and the Sylphor to give Arielle the time to finish her transformation.

Once it was complete, Arielle gave a hearty tug to snap the ropes binding her. She then ran over to Noah and quickly pulled his sword out of its sheath.

Knocking Elizabeth savagely down, Emmanuel turned to face Arielle. The two sized each other up for a second, and then hurled themselves at one another. Their swords clanged with supernatural intensity.

"I'm going to kill you!" Arielle screamed.

"You're too late! I'm already dead!" yelled Emmanuel.

Brother and sister assailed one another mercilessly, weaving their deadly dance back and forth across the basement, keeping time with the metallic ring of their glowing blades as they clashed and clashed again. After several minutes of combat, Emmanuel's strength began to win out over Arielle's agility, despite the ferociousness of the girl's attack. The Dark Elf took advantage of a momentary opening in Arielle's defence and bombarded her weapon with powerful swings in an attempt to bat it aside. When he finally succeeded, he closed quickly and punched her in the face. Crying out in pain, Arielle stumbled backwards, her concentration broken. Emmanuel pressed his advantage, disarming her with a series of mighty blows.

"Finish this!" yelled Saddington, who had gotten to her feet during the fight. "Kill her, Mastermyrr!"

Emmanuel pointed his sword at Arielle's throat and made her kneel down in front of him. Though still reeling from Emmanuel's savage assault earlier, Elizabeth tried to get to her feet, but the sorceress would not be caught flatfooted a second time. A ball of mystic fire struck Elizabeth in the chest, sending her flying into the wall head-first. The poor girl fell to the ground, unconscious.

The Dark Elf's blade was now pointing at Arielle's throat. He could have killed her with a flick of his wrist if he wanted to.

"What are you waiting for, Mastermyrr?" growled the old woman impatiently. "This is no way for the Voivod of the New World Clans to act!"

The teenaged boy did not reply, but neither did he give any sign that he would obey his grandmother. For the time being, he was satisfied with simply preventing Arielle from taking action by holding his sword to her neck.

"I loved our mother, but she chose to save *you* and abandon *me*," he snarled, his eyes filled with hate. "I was raised by Dark Elves and Necromancers and Kobolds. Do you have any idea what that means?"

Arielle could feel his pain, as well as his hesitation about what to do with her. Would he kill her or spare her?

"I'm sorry, Emmanuel. I'm sure our mother loved you very much."

Saddington sighed in exasperation. Stretching a hand towards Arielle, she spoke more words of power, "*Erini statuere ternitas!*"

A globe of light slowly expanded in the witch's palm.

"There are some spells I like much more than others," she chuckled as she teased the globe with her fingers. "How would you like to be turned into stone? To spend eternity as a statue?"

The beam of light snaked towards Arielle, who stared in horror at her glowing doom.

"Hey!" boomed a voice from behind Emmanuel. He whipped around—and came face-to-face with Elliot, who was holding a piece of rope in one hand. "I want my Nikes back!"

Elliot punched Emmanuel in the face as hard as he could. The other boy fell backwards, landing between Arielle and the beam of light. Instead of striking its intended target, the beam hit Emmanuel directly in the chest. He immediately stiffened, his skin hardening and taking on the greyish hue of stone.

"That guy's got a steel jaw," Elliot winced, rubbing his knuckles.

Not wasting a moment, Arielle sprang into action. Scooping up Emmanuel's sword, which had fallen on the floor, she bounded over to Saddington and plunged the weapon into the old woman's chest.

Saddington's eyes widened in surprise. She tried to pull the sword out, but her efforts proved fruitless. Her face twisting in pain, the witch staggered forward before falling to her knees. She looked at Arielle for a second, swayed for another, and then dropped on her face in the dirt. Her shrivelled form twitched briefly and was still.

Arielle ran over to Noah, who was lying on his back. He was not moving. There was an ugly wound in his chest, and his clothes were soaked in blood.

"I'm going to find a phone to call for help!" yelled Elliot after checking to see that Elizabeth was OK.

"Hurry, Eli!" Arielle urged him.

"I'll be right back!" he said, sprinting up the stairs.

"Noah, it's me," whispered Arielle, bending over the wounded teenager. "Can you hear me?"

She placed a hand on his forehead; his skin was cold and damp.

"Noah, please! Say something!"

Tears rolled down her cheeks and dripped onto Noah's pale face.

"Arielle…" he mumbled.

"I'm right here."

"Did…we win?"

"Yes, we did. Saddington is dead!"

"And Emmanuel?"

"He's going to spend eternity as a statue," Arielle replied, echoing Saddington's words.

Noah glanced down at his bloody shirt.

"Nasty cut," he said weakly.

Arielle held him tenderly.

"Don't worry. Help will be here soon," she reassured him.

Noah smiled.

"Your eyes," he whispered. "They're different. I've never seen eyes the colour of honey before."

The injured youth's breathing became shallow as he began to drown in his own blood.

"Don't leave me," he choked out the words.

He began to wheeze as he shut his eyes. His head felt heavy on Arielle's shoulder.

"Look at me, Noah," she pleaded.

Forcing his eyes open one last time, Noah looked at Arielle.

"Kiss me," he said faintly.

Without hesitation, she pressed her lips to his.

A series of flashbacks tumbled through her mind, like the first time they had kissed in the motel. The images gradually came into focus. Arielle was no longer in Saddington's basement, but was running through a forest, trying to escape from someone. Though Elleira was in control of her body, she was aware of what was going on. Glancing over her shoulder, she saw the lights of Bombyx Manor and could hear screaming in the distance. This must be the night the Dark Elves had attacked the Alters in the ballroom! But that happened two days ago, the first time Arielle had ever visited the manor.

She noticed something moving nearby.

"Come back here!" Emmanuel shouted at her.

Arielle recalled Noah's words, *"Emmanuel wasn't trying to save you, Arielle—he was trying to get the pendant."*

Elleira tried to distance herself from Emmanuel, but

could not. Her love for Noah had weakened her, making her unable to run faster or fly.

Emmanuel was catching up to her and would overtake her in a matter of seconds. Suddenly, Noah reared out of the bushes behind them and tackled the other boy. The two grappled one another on the forest floor.

"Go on, get out of here!" Noah yelled at Elleira. "Run to Gleason Road!"

Elleira nodded. She pulled the pendant out of her pocket and hung it around her neck. As she turned to flee, she glanced over her shoulder and saw Emmanuel headbutt Noah, stunning him. Emmanuel threw the other boy off and got to his feet. Elleira increased her speed.

It was at this moment that Arielle remembered taking control of her body.

"*Too weak*," said a voice inside Arielle's head. "*Too weak to fly.*"

Arielle ran through the dark forest, not following any path. She was out of breath and her legs ached. She could hear yelling behind her, and barking even farther away.

"Run, Arielle! Run!" shouted Noah.

There was a flash.

The trees disappeared, only to be replaced by the walls of Glory High. Arielle was revisiting an even older incident from her past. It was her first day of high school. She was hurrying to her English class, her head bent and arms full of books. Lea Darling followed behind, making fun of her behind her back. As Lea moved forward to make Arielle drop her books, Noah grabbed Lea's arm and dragged her back. "Go pick on someone else!" he hissed in the blond girl's ear.

Arielle was amazed. This new flashback allowed her to witness an event from her very own life from a different perspective.

Another flash.

And then another. They kept coming and coming. Each one involved Noah making someone stop teasing or hurting her, always in a manner that had originally escaped Arielle's notice. There were so many of these flashes—at elementary school, at high school, in public— that she lost count.

The last flash was about an incident that happened in a schoolyard. Arielle felt the warmth of the autumn sun caress her skin. A group of students was gathered near a grown-up she recognized as her fourth-grade gym teacher. The students were divided into two teams. Drawing closer, Arielle watched Richard walk over to a little girl with red hair and a face full of freckles. This little girl was the only one who had not been chosen by either side, so she stood apart from the others. Alone.

"You can have her!" shouted Richard, giving the girl a dirty look.

The other children burst out laughing. The little red-headed girl hung her head in shame. The humiliation bit as deeply now as it had then.

Arielle scanned the crowd for Simon Vanesse. This was when he was supposed to defend her. She finally spotted him, standing with his arms crossed in front of Noah. Strangely, though, he was laughing along with all of the other students—all, that is, except one.

"Richard, leave her be!" a child's voice called out.

The voice was not Simon's, but Noah's. Arielle knelt by the side of Noah as a little boy. He had the scar on his cheek, even back then. She studied his features and smiled at him.

"I always thought Simon was the one who stood up for me that day," she said. "Why didn't you tell me that it had been you?"

She leaned forward and kissed his cheek. Noah

smiled back, and then grabbed a ball and ran over to start the game.

Images began spinning in her mind again, so fast it was making her dizzy. There was an explosion of light, followed by utter darkness. Arielle could once more feel Noah's lips against hers. Opening her eyes, she saw she was in Saddington's basement.

Noah lay still in her arms.

"I saw everything you did," she murmured. "I had been so infatuated with Simon all these years, I never realized you were looking out for me. I'm sorry."

The young man weakly raised a hand to stroke her hair.

"You can't leave me now," she said, taking his hand. "I need you."

"If there is a way to come back, I'll find it," he promised her.

Tears flowed once more down Arielle's cheeks. She did not want to lose Noah. The two of them would never have the chance to explore their relationship. It wasn't fair!

"*In this world, the body is only an anchor for the soul,*" a voice whispered in her mind. It was the same unknown voice that had spoken to her that afternoon.

Arielle knew she had to repeat these words to Noah.

"The body is only an anchor for the soul," she blurted out. "Remember, the body is only an anchor for the soul."

"I'll remember."

"Sooner or later, I would have fallen in love with you, Noah Davidoff," she said, caressing the scar on Noah's cheek with her finger.

"I know, Venus…"

He smiled at her once more, and closed his eyes.

And lay deathly still…

CHAPTER 31

Elizabeth's father's minivan headed down Gleason Road towards Bombyx Manor.

Elliot was behind the wheel, and Arielle was sitting beside him. She was in her Dayform now. She had removed her pendant and had changed into her regular clothes.

"We're almost there," said Elliot.

Arielle did not respond. She kept thinking about her decision to leave Noah back in the basement. It had been the hardest thing she had ever had to do in her life. The evening's events at Saddington's house played in an endless loop in her mind…

"IT'S over," Elliot said quietly. "I called 9-1-1. Help will be here soon."

Her face streaked with tears, Arielle hugged Noah's body until Elliot gently pried her arms away from the dead youth.

"It's never going to be over," sobbed Arielle. "The Alters and the Elves will never leave us alone."

She bent over to kiss Noah's forehead, and then stood up.

"We're going to put an end to this!" Arielle said firmly.

"What?" asked Elliot. "How?"

The young woman glanced down at Emmanuel's petrified form.

"In any way we can," she replied, picking up an old blanket draped over some furniture. "I'll need your help getting him out of here."

"Who? Emmanuel?!? You're nuts! He's been changed into solid stone! He must weigh a ton!"

"Grab the dolly from under the stairs," Arielle continued, ignoring the boy's protests. "It'll come in handy."

The two of them lugged Emmanuel out of the basement and placed him in the minivan. They had just enough time to duck behind the neighbour's hedge as the ambulance came into view. After watching the ambulance attendants enter the house, Arielle and Elliot quickly drove off in the minivan. They made a quick stop at the Queen and Rivard residences to pick up a change of clothing for each of them before heading to the manor with their unusual cargo.

ARIELLE'S glanced at her watch: it was 5 a.m. The sun would be up soon.

"I hope this works," muttered Elliot.

"Me, too," added Arielle, who was examining Noah's pendant, which she had found on the floor near Emmanuel's petrified hand. She planned on using it to save everyone she cared about, or, at the very least, buy them some peace for a while.

"How do you know if your uncle and the Animalters are still alive?"

"The Alters wouldn't hurt them," Arielle said hopefully. "They need them as hostages to trade for the pendants."

The minivan drove between the rows of maple trees lining the private lane leading to the manor. All traces of the battle that had occurred there a few hours ago had been erased.

Elliot parked the minivan by the terrace and turned off the engine. The two youths looked at each other for a moment. Arielle nodded; she was ready.

Dozens of Alters had gathered upon the terrace as soon as the minivan had come into view. They watched the vehicle suspiciously.

Arielle opened the door and got out. Elliot did likewise, taking care to avoid making any sudden moves. He slowly walked around the minivan to stand next to Arielle. Sword in hand, the Alters rushed down the stairs to surround the teenagers.

"I want to speak to your leader!" Arielle shouted, shielding her eyes from the dazzling light of the glowing draugur swords.

The Alters glanced at one another uncertainly.

"Where is Reivax?" she demanded.

A voice from the rear of the group barked a command, and the Alters parted to reveal Reivax, the Alter of Xavier Vanesse, standing at the foot of the stairs. By his side were Ael and Nomis's raven Animalter.

"Here I am, girl!" Reivax boomed. "What do you want?"

"I want to propose a truce," replied Arielle.

The old Alter laughed.

"A truce?"

"Noah Davidoff is dead," she said stiffly, masking her

grief.

"And your point is?" asked Ael.

"As you know, the prophecy can only come true if both Valinn are alive. But that is no longer the case. The only thing you have to worry about now is the Dark Elves coming after you. You may think they have all been destroyed, but that's not true. Falko's heir, Mastermyrr, is still alive!"

Arielle turned to Elliot, who slid open the minivan's side door. The rear seats had been removed to make room for a large object covered by an old blanket. With a nod from Arielle, Elliot yanked the blanket off to reveal the life-sized statue of Emmanuel.

"Ladies and gentlemen, I present Mastermyrr, Falko's heir and the Voivod of the New World Clans!" announced Arielle with a dramatic flourish. "He was accidentally transformed into stone by Saddington herself!"

Reivax briefly examined the statue.

"This—thing—has a certain value," he agreed, "but not enough for me to keep listening. Dispose of them!"

The Alters raised their weapons and advanced menacingly.

"Wait!" called Arielle. She raised her hand and presented Noah's half-moon pendant. "Wouldn't *this* have a certain value as well?"

The approaching force stopped as one man, all eyes glued to the moon-shaped pendant. Arielle addressed her captive audience.

"Saddington made it clear to me that necromancers and Dark Elves from the other clans would soon be sending reinforcements to help Mastermyrr. But without this," she shook the pendant for emphasis, "it will be nearly impossible for them to defeat you."

Reivax was hypnotized by the piece of jewellery dangling from Arielle's hand.

"Very well, young lady," Reivax's eyes were filled with the desire to own this invaluable prize. "What do you want in exchange for the pendant?"

"I want you to release my uncle and the Animalters. And I want you to let me and my friends live in Glory without having to worry about the Alters coming after us."

Reivax mulled over the girl's proposal.

"Agreed! We have a deal! Give me the pendant, and I will release your friends."

Arielle hesitated for a second before tossing the pendant to Reivax. The raven Animalter leaped into the air and assumed bird form the instant the piece of jewellery left her hand. The bird caught the pendant in its beak, circled the esplanade and landed on Reivax's forearm, which he had extended as a perch. The raven dropped the pendant into the Alter's palm.

"Let's kill her now!" yelled Ael, drawing her sword.

Reivax raised a hand. "Not so fast! Where is the second pendant?"

"I hid it," said Arielle. "I am the only one who knows where it is. If the Alters ever come after me or my friends, then I will give it to the Elves. I'm hanging on to it as insurance."

"Don't you trust me?" he asked, motioning for Ael to sheathe her weapon.

"No," replied Arielle coolly. "Not in the least."

REIVAX HAD THE ALTERS bring the statue of Emmanuel into the manor's large library.

"Is he still alive?" Ael eyed the stone form as it was carried past.

"Maybe we'll find out one day," replied the were-raven, who had assumed human form.

Reivax walked Arielle and Elliot back to the minivan.

"Falko killed my heir," he told the teenagers. "Now, thanks to you, Falko's heir will have a special place among my hunting trophies. I will be able to admire this statue for the rest of my life."

Reivax looked towards the garage and snapped his fingers. One of the doors rose, revealing six Alters.

"Bring the prisoners!" ordered Reivax.

Yvan and the Animalters were immediately marched across the esplanade.

"The Alters will not bother you anymore," Reivax assured her. "You may continue to live in Glory. I will uphold my part of the bargain as long as the second pendant is kept safe. But should you ever lose it or it falls into the hands of the Sylphors, our deal will be null and void. Is that clear?"

"Absolutely," said Arielle.

"One last thing. Be sure to tell me if the Elves start bothering you again. It will be a pleasure for me to take care of them—personally."

"If they do, you'll be the first to know."

Reivax tipped his head in greeting and headed back to the manor with the man-raven. Ael gave Arielle a withering look.

"I'll be keeping an eye on you, Pumpkin!" she spat out the words.

Arielle met the other girl's gaze without flinching.

"Me too, *Dahling*!"

Ael spun on her heel and stomped off without another word.

"Mistress!" called Brutus.

The Alters had escorted the hostages halfway across the esplanade before withdrawing to the garage. Yvan had raced ahead of the Animalters, arms outstretched.

"I was so worried about you!" he gushed, hugging his

niece. "Are you all right?"

This sudden display of affection surprised Arielle. Her uncle had never been much of the touchy-feely type.

"I'm OK," she said.

"Thanks for playing your get-out-of-jail card for us," Brutus smiled in relief.

"Seriously, though, what did you do to get them to let us go?" asked Geri, giving the were-cat a dirty look.

"It's a long story," she told the DoberMan.

"Um, where's Noah?" Freki spoke up.

Arielle fell silent and glanced at Elliot, who lowered his head. Judging by the pair's reaction, it was clear to Freki and the others that something terrible had happened. Geri seemed particularly shaken.

"Do you mean that…" he began.

Arielle swallowed hard before answering.

"Noah is dead, Geri."

"No!" exclaimed the DoberMan. "It can't be! He's tougher than any of us!"

"He was brave, right until the end," Arielle added softly.

Overwhelmed with grief, Geri could only nod sadly. Freki draped a sympathetic arm around the other were-dog's shoulders.

"We have to go home now," said Yvan. "It'll be dawn soon. We have some wounds that need to be tended to."

"But Geri and I have nowhere to go," Freki said.

Arielle's eyes met her uncle's. He could tell what she was thinking and winked at her to give his consent.

"You can stay with us," Arielle suggested with a smile.

Elliot got behind the wheel and started the engine. The others followed in silence, with Geri bringing up the rear. As soon as he had closed the side door, the minivan headed off across the esplanade towards the laneway leading to Gleason Road.

"Are you serious? Are the mutts really going to live with us on Sphinx Street?" Brutus grumbled.

As they drove into town, the first rays of sunlight peeked over the horizon, indicating the start of a new day.

CHAPTER 32

Reivax made sure the Alter deaths…

…were blamed on two fiery traffic accidents that had claimed the lives of several of the town's youth and seniors. The victims' bodies had been burned and mangled beyond recognition, masking their true cause of death. In a matter of days, the various loose ends had been neatly tied up, and the file on all this Alter business was quietly closed.

The last of the funerals was that of the two teenaged princes of Glory High School. Noah's parents had requested that their son be buried next to his best friend, Simon, in the Vanesse family vault.

It was a gorgeous morning. The sun shone warm and bright in the cloudless sky, taking some of the bite out of the nippy November wind. Lea Darling and Xavier Vanesse walked with the boys' families at the head of the funeral procession, while Arielle and her friends followed behind with the other mourners. If Lea's and Xavier's Alters were controlling their Dayforms through integral possession, it was impossible to tell.

Once at the vault, Arielle, Rose and Elliot moved away from the crowd to stand to one side. Yvan joined them, holding the leashed Dobermans in one hand and carrying Brutus in the crook of his other arm. Arielle took her cat from her uncle. She began to stroke an uncharacteristically docile Brutus.

Of all of Arielle's friends, only Elizabeth was absent. She had been hospitalized with a rare type of septicemia, a form of blood poisoning that, fortunately, could be treated with intravenous antibiotics. There was no doubt that Elizabeth's medical condition was a result of the attempt to change her into a Kobold. Elizabeth would have to stay at the hospital under observation for a few more days. Hopefully, the treatment would rid her of every trace of Kobold and make her entirely human once more.

"My friends, it is normal that we feel sad," said the priest. "We have suffered a great loss. Simon Vanesse and Noah Davidoff were remarkable young men, greatly admired and loved by their families and friends."

A number of people began sobbing. The priest looked at the mourners with compassion.

"Today, we seek comfort in love. The love of our family and friends, but also the love that Simon and Noah brought into our lives every day. Though these two young men have left us, they continue to live on in our hearts. We are gathered here this morning to see them to their final rest, and also to tell them that we will never forget them. They will need all of our love and strength in the kingdom beyond."

At the end of the service, the mourners expressed their condolences to the boys' families and walked quietly away. Rose and Elliot joined the crowd leaving the cemetery, but Arielle did not.

"Are you coming?" asked Yvan.

"I'd like to stay here for a bit with Brutus and the dogs," she replied.

"All right. I'll wait for you in the car."

Yvan gave her a sympathetic smile and left.

Arielle was now alone in front of the vault with Xavier and several funeral home employees. The old man laid his hand on Simon's coffin one final time and lowered his head. After a few moments, he told the employees to place the two coffins in the vault. Once this was done, the employees exited the vault, clanging the metal gate shut behind them. It was at this point that Geri and Freki began to howl. Arielle's heart clenched; she understood and shared their grief.

"Goodbye, Noah," she whispered.

She wiped her eyes and made to leave. Just then, Simon's raven Animalter soared into view. It circled the vault several times, gave a loud, mournful cry and flew away into the mountains.

THE NEXT DAY, Arielle was back at school. Morning classes had been cancelled owing to meetings with grief counsellors, but those for the rest of the day were still on. Arielle met up with Rose and Elliot at lunch.

"I got my Nikes back," said Elliot as he showed off his footwear. "The owner of the Apollo Motel found them in one of the rooms."

"That's great," said Arielle without enthusiasm.

Rose placed her hand on Arielle's.

"Are you OK?" she asked, concerned.

Arielle nodded silently.

ARIELLE barely ate anything at lunch. Returning to class was very difficult for her; it was like she lost any motivation to be at school. In English class, Arielle sat at the back of the room instead of in her usual seat.

"You don't usually hide back there, Ms. Queen,"

remarked Mr. Gordon.

Arielle simply shrugged. Looking down at her textbook, she read and re-read the title, *Dr. Jekyll and Mr. Hyde*, like a mantra, fighting the urge to burst into tears. Her throat clenched and her heart ached—she missed Elizabeth and Noah desperately.

"A few days ago, one of you asked me what would happen if you separated good from evil," said Mr. Gordon to the class.

The students nodded.

"Well, now that you've read the book, you should be able to answer that question. Ms. Queen, how about you?"

"I haven't finished it yet, sir," said Arielle.

The teacher smiled at her.

"Anyone else?"

No-one spoke.

"I will quote you a passage from the last chapter. Here is what Jekyll has to say about the good and evil in all of us. *If each, I told myself, could be housed in separate identities, life would be relieved of all that was unbearable; the unjust might go his way, delivered from the aspirations and remorse of his more upright twin; and the just could walk steadfastly and securely on his upward path, doing the good things in which he found his pleasure, and no longer exposed to disgrace and penitence by the hands of this extraneous evil. It was the curse of mankind that these incongruous faggots were thus bound together—that in the agonised womb of consciousness, these polar twins should be continuously struggling.*"

Mr. Gordon closed the book and addressed the class once more.

"So, do you agree with Jekyll that this co-existence of good and evil is a curse? And would we truly be free if we could separate these two opposite personalities?"

Again, silence. Arielle finally raised her hand.

"Separating good and evil means separating joy and sorrow, kindness and cruelty, and worst of all, love and hate." Images of Noah and Emmanuel popped into her head. "When that happens, we stop being human and turn into something else, something horrible."

Arielle took a moment to compose herself before going on.

"And that is the real curse."

CHAPTER 33

The first thing Arielle noticed when she got home was that her uncle had already started drinking.

He was taking sips from his glass of red wine as he set the table. It wasn't his first glass, either; the bottle on the counter was almost empty. Arielle placed her schoolbag on a chair and poured herself some juice.

"Doesn't that smell great?" called Yvan, taking a casserole dish out of the oven.

"Are those cabbage rolls?" asked Arielle, sniffing the air.

"Yes, ma'am!"

Yvan put the dish on the table.

"Juliette prepared them just for you." Yvan refilled his glass. "How did it go at school?"

Arielle shrugged.

"I don't know who to trust anymore," she replied glumly as she sat at the table. "I have the impression that everyone I meet is an Alter and that they're all watching me."

"There's nothing to worry about during the day," Yvan

assured his niece. "Don't forget that an Alter can only take control of his host when the host is asleep. If the host is awake, the Alter can't do anything."

"What about integral possession?"

"As far as I know, only members of powerful Alter families, like the Vanesses, can do that."

Yvan served Arielle some cabbage rolls and mashed potatoes.

"Go on, eat. You'll feel better," he urged her.

"I'm not really hungry."

Arielle fidgeted with her fork for a few seconds before adding, "Uncle Yvan, did my mother love me?"

"Of course she did."

"Did she suffer when she died?"

Yvan looked away and cringed. Arielle's question forced him to recall many painful memories.

"The car had burst into flames," Yvan's tone was wooden. "There were Dark Elves everywhere. The only thing I clearly remember was running away with you in my arms."

"What about Emmanuel? Did my mother love him, too?"

Yvan let out a heavy sigh.

"It was different with Emmanuel. He was closer to Erik than to Gabrielle."

"Why did she abandon him?"

"Abandoning your brother was a decision that ripped Gabrielle's heart out, but it was one she had to make to save you."

Arielle nodded half-heartedly, and then rose. She hadn't touched her food.

"I'm tired," she said, grabbing her bag. "I'm going to bed."

Yvan did not object. Clearly, the thing she needed most right now was to get some rest. After Arielle had climbed the stairs to her bedroom, Yvan got up and took another bottle of wine from the cellar.

ARIELLE WAS HAPPY to see Geri and Freki, who were lying at the foot of her bed. They rose to greet her, tails wagging. The young girl set her bag down and marched straight to the closet. She pushed aside her regular clothes, found the yellow butterfly and pressed it. The hidden panel in the back wall slid open. *My very own Batcave,* she thought.

She first checked that the pendant was still safely where she had hidden it. She then went through her Alter outfits and adjusted them on their hangers. Examining her arsenal, she decided that although acidus injectors were great for fighting Sylphors, she preferred her trusty draugur sword. Satisfied that her equipment was in top shape, she shut the secret closet and stretched out on her bed. Brutus hopped up to join her.

"Hey, you," she greeted Brutus with a pat on the head. "The Dobermans haven't been giving you a hard time, have they?"

Brutus arched his back and hissed at the dogs, which immediately began barking.

"OK, OK, guys, I get it! How about a truce for tonight? I really have to get some rest."

The Animalters finally settled down.

"Thanks," she mumbled into her pillow. Brutus curled up beside her and purred, knowing that would help her doze off. Arielle couldn't keep her eyes open one second more. An image of Noah Davidoff popped into her mind.

"I hope that you're in a better place now," Arielle whispered before nodding off.

ARIELLE found herself drifting in darkness. Gradually,

colours and vague forms began to appear. As things came into focus, she could make out various objects in her surroundings.

She was standing by a window in a small, rundown apartment with shabby furniture. Looking outside, she could see she was in a city, but did not recognize the skyline. The nearby buildings were all heavily damaged, with crumbling façades and holes in the walls and roofs. The city had been devastated by either an earthquake or a war—probably the latter, judging by the smell of smoke and gunpowder in the air.

"Arielle," called a voice from behind her.

The red-headed girl spun around. A young woman of Arielle's age was standing in the middle of the room.

"We don't have a lot of time," said the stranger. "The sun is about to set."

There was a certain resemblance between Arielle and the woman, who was wearing leather clothing similar to an Alter's outfit. However, the style was dated, like something from the nineteen forties or fifties.

"Who are you?" gasped Arielle.

"I'm Abigaël, your grandmother."

This girl, her grandmother? No way!

"My grandmother is dead," said Arielle warily.

"I will die one day, that's true, but hopefully not today," Abigaël replied.

Arielle looked around the room. "Where are we?"

"Berlin. In 1945," said Abigaël.

"Is this a dream?"

"No. We are really speaking to one another. I am contacting you from the past."

"Oh, really?"

"In this world, the body is only an anchor for the soul. Once you raise the anchor, the soul can spread its wings and fly to any world it wants," explained Abigaël.

That was what the voice I heard say just before Noah died! Arielle's eyes widened in recognition. "You're the one who spoke to me when I was in the basement of Saddington's house, aren't you?"

"Ties of the spirit are sometimes as strong as ties of blood, you know."

Arielle turned around to look out the window once more. The buildings seemed to be in as bad shape as ones she had seen in photographs of World War II that her history teacher, Mr. Gravel, had shown the class once.

"I can't believe I am really in 1945!" she marvelled.

"Now listen to me, Arielle." The young woman's tone became grave. "I have to talk to you about the prophecy. We could not beat the Sylphors and Alters—there were too many of them. If everything has been going to plan, you are humanity's new hope. The prophecy says that before the Valinn can go to the Land of the Dead to fight Loki and Hel, they must defeat every Sylphor and Alter here on Earth. That is what you have to do. But you won't be able to do it alone."

"It's too late," Arielle added sadly. "Noah is dead."

"What's with the long face?" said Abigaël. "Things aren't always what they seem. It's important you keep believing that anything is possible. You are the one who will make the prophecy come true, and no-one else. But you will need help."

"Noah is the only one who could have helped me," said Arielle.

"You're forgetting about the six protectors from the prophecy," the young woman pointed out. "One of them is Jason Thorn. He is an Elding Knight who was taken prisoner by the Sylphors a few days ago. Mikael and I tried to rescue him. We failed."

Abigaël was undoubtedly referring to Mikael Davidoff, Noah's grandfather. Was her grandmother in love with Mikael? *It would fit the pattern,* Arielle thought dryly.

"I don't have a lot of time," Abigaël went on, "the Elves know where I am. Listen, Jason is still being held prisoner by the Elves in 2006. You must rescue him."

"Why? What does he have to do with me?" asked Arielle.

"Jason Thorn is the only one who knows where you can find the Vade-Mekum, a book that can tell you how to contact the spirits of our ancestors. You will need it to defeat the demons," said Abigaël.

"But the Elves have been keeping Jason locked up for sixty years. He must be dead by now!" exclaimed Arielle.

"Those who are under the protection of the Valkyries have special powers," replied Abigaël. "You will understand one day."

"Where should I start looking for him?"

As Abigaël began to speak, the door to her apartment burst open. A dozen uniformed men—actually Dark Elves dressed like German soldiers—charged into the room and set upon the young woman. Arielle wanted to help her grandmother, but found she could not move from the window.

More Sylphors poured into the room. Despite her brave struggle, Abigaël was clearly outmatched.

"Don't forget his name!" Abigaël shouted. "Jason Thorn! He's called Jason Thorn! He's being held prisoner with your mother! They're at Orfray, in the Pit of the Carrion Eaters!"

"What?! My mother's alive?"

One of the Sylphors drew a draugur dagger from his uniform and snuck up behind Abigaël.

"Look out! Behind you!" shouted Arielle.

But Abigaël chose to look at her granddaughter rather than deal with her attacker. Arielle was pulled away into the darkness before she had a chance to learn whether Abigaël was able to avoid the fatal blow.

"SHE'S ALIVE!" YELLED ARIELLE, instantly awake.

The girl's cry woke Brutus and the Dobermans. In a flash, Arielle bounded out of bed and ran to the secret closet. She quickly put on an Alter outfit, hung the half-moon pendant around her neck and grabbed her weapons.

Yvan swung the bedroom door open as his niece was speaking the magic words that would allow her to assume her Alter form, "Fra Retla! Fra Alter!"

"What's going on?" asked Uncle Yvan, who was slightly out of breath from having sprinted to Arielle's room.

"She's alive!" repeated Arielle as she underwent her Altermorphosis. "My mother is alive!"

Once in her new form, Arielle strapped the draugur sword to her waist and the acidus injectors to her belt.

"Who told you that?" Yvan was confused.

"My grandmother. She spoke to me when I was sleeping. She said that the Sylphors were keeping her and this Elding Knight prisoner in some kind of pit. I think she called it Orphrase."

"Orfray," corrected Yvan.

"You heard of it?" Arielle stared at her uncle in amazement.

"Yes, but it's a long story," he added.

He removed a flask from his pocket and raised it to his lips. Before he could take a swig, however, Arielle shot across the room with superhuman speed and grabbed his hand.

"What are you doing?" she scolded him as she snatched

the flask away. "This isn't the time to be drinking! My mother needs us! We have to rescue her right away!"

Yvan did not respond.

"Why do you drink so much, anyway?" Arielle asked. She was determined to get a straight answer from her uncle this time, no matter what!

"Tell me!"

"I think it's time you learned the truth," said Yvan quietly.

"The truth? What 'truth'?"

Yvan walked down the hall to the bathroom and shut the door. About ten minutes later, he walked into Arielle's room, wiping his face with the towel draped around his neck.

"There are three ways to neutralize an Alter if you are a Hugar Numinn," he said. "By wearing a half-moon pendant, by not falling asleep or by getting drunk. Since I don't have a pendant and I need to sleep, I decided to get drunk instead."

He pulled the towel away from his face. His beard was gone. This was the first time Arielle had ever seen her uncle clean-shaven. As she studied his features, she realized he looked familiar. The peculiar scar on his right cheek, previously hidden by the beard, was exactly like the one on...

"Noah?" Arielle was stunned.

She then remembered what Elleira had told her when she was hidden in the forest near Bombyx Manor that first night. *Noah's real name is Nazar Ivanovitch Davidoff. Ivanovitch...Yvan...*

Arielle's eyes grew wide as she made the connection. Her mind was reeling. She leaned against the wall for support, her knees trembling.

"Uncle Yvan. You're—Noah!? How is that possible?"

The stern look on his face softened. As he looked at

Arielle, her last doubts about her uncle's identity vanished. Those were definitely the eyes of Noah Davidoff.

"I told you if I could find a way to come back, I would. Well, Venus, I did find a way. There's just one problem: I came back twenty-five years too early."

TO BE CONTINUED.....

ABOUT THE AUTHOR

Born in 1971 in the Laurentides of Quebec, MICHEL J. LÉVESQUE began his career publishing his particular brand of science fiction and fantasy in a number of magazines including *Solaris* from Quebec and *Galaxies* from France. *Samuel de la chasse-galerie* (Médiaspaul, 2006), his first novel was listed in 2006-2007 by *Communication-Jeunesse* and was a finalist for the *Cécile-Gagnon* prize. The *Prix jeunesse de science-fiction et de fantastique québécois* also shortlisted the work. *Arielle Queen, La société secrète des alters* (A Knight for a Queen, in English) was nominated for the 25th Edition of the *prix du Public La Presse* Prize, was *volet littéraire* at the Salon du livre of Montréal in 2007 and was nominated for the Aurora 2008 Award for best French language book.

ABOUT THE TRANSLATOR

GREG KELM is a freelance translator with 15 years' experience and a degree in French to English translation from Glendon College. Greg currently lectures in English translation at Laval University in Quebec City and is working on, among other projects, the translation of the complete Arielle Queen series.

9 781926 716329